"What is it about you that keeps me so confused?" Noah asked.

Starr couldn't be sure, but she suspected his confusion was caused by his intellect arguing with male instinct. On a purely rational level he obviously didn't want to get involved with her. But on a physical level…maybe he wasn't so sure. A small, embarrassed smile tugged at her lips—it was flattering, even though she didn't want to get involved, either. But what was so wrong with her, anyway?

"For the record…" she said thoughtfully. "What do you dislike about me? I mean, aside from my impulsiveness?"

"You want some kind of list?" he asked, giving her a teasing grin.

"Just hit the high points," she said with an overdose of sweetness.

"Er…I don't dislike you. But we've got different priorities. I have Becky to think of…."

Starr blinked. She respected Noah's protectiveness toward his niece. Yet she couldn't help thinking he was looking for an excuse. Not so much to keep her out of his niece's life, but out of *his*.

Dear Reader,

Silhouette Romance is celebrating the month of valentines with six very special love stories—and three brand-new miniseries you don't want to miss. *On Baby Patrol,* our BUNDLE OF JOY selection, by bestselling author Sharon De Vita, is book one of her wonderful series, LULLABIES AND LOVE, about a legendary cradle that brings love to three brothers who are officers of the law.

In *Granted: Big Sky Groom,* Carol Grace begins her sparkling new series, BEST-KEPT WISHES, in which three high school friends' prom-night wishes are finally about to be granted. Author Julianna Morris tells the delightful story of a handsome doctor whose life is turned topsy-turvy when he becomes the guardian of his orphaned niece in *Dr. Dad.* And in Cathleen Galitz's spirited tale, *100% Pure Cowboy,* a woman returns home from a mother-daughter bonding trip with the husband of her dreams.

Next is *Corporate Groom,* which starts Linda Varner's terrific new miniseries, THREE WEDDINGS AND A FAMILY, about long-lost relatives who find a family. And finally, in *With This Child...,* Sally Carleen tells the compelling story of a woman whose baby was switched at birth—and the single father who will do anything to keep his child.

I hope you enjoy all six of Silhouette Romance's love stories this month. And next month, in March, be sure to look for *The Princess Bride* by bestselling author Diana Palmer, which launches Silhouette Romance's new monthly promotional miniseries, VIRGIN BRIDES.

Regards,

Joan Marlow Golan
Senior Editor

Please address questions and book requests to:
Silhouette Reader Service
U.S.: 3010 Walden Ave., P.O. Box 1325, Buffalo, NY 14269
Canadian: P.O. Box 609, Fort Erie, Ont. L2A 5X3

DR. DAD

Julianna Morris

Silhouette

R O M A N C E™

Published by Silhouette Books

America's Publisher of Contemporary Romance

In memory of my grandfathers—
Virgil and Daniel—two remarkable men
who passed on a commitment to ideals,
strength of purpose and the joy of laughter.

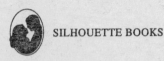 SILHOUETTE BOOKS

ISBN 0-373-19278-9

DR. DAD

Copyright © 1998 by Martha Ann Ford

Printed in U.S.A.

JULIANNA MORRIS

has an offbeat sense of humor that frequently gets her into trouble. She is often accused of being curious about everything—her interests ranging from oceanography and photography to traveling, antiquing, walking on the beach and reading science fiction. Choosing a college major was extremely difficult, but after many changes she earned a bachelor's degree in environmental science.

Julianna's writing is supervised by a cat named Gandalf, who sits on the computer monitor and criticizes each keystroke. Ultimately she would like a home overlooking the ocean, where she can write to her heart's content—and Gandalf's malcontent. She'd like to share that home with her own romantic hero—someone with a warm, sexy smile, lots of patience and an offbeat sense of humor to match her own. Oh, yes…and he has to like cats.

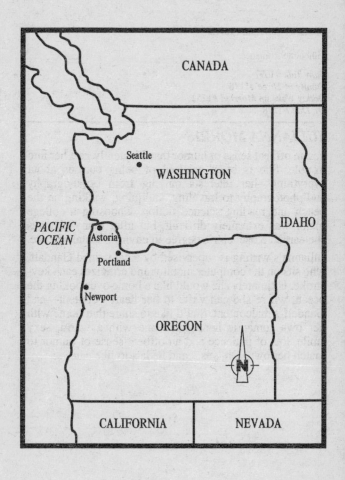

Chapter One

The wail of fire engine sirens cut through the calm morning and Starr automatically pulled to one side of the road. Several trucks and police vehicles sped around her, headed for a rising plume of smoke on the hillside.

Alarmed, Starr followed the flashing lights and slammed to a stop outside the perimeter established by the emergency personnel. Heart sinking, she grabbed her notebook and confirmed the address; sure enough, this was the house belonging to her goddaughter's baby-sitter.

"Blast," she muttered, jumping out of the car.

"Sorry, lady, you'll have to stay back like everyone else," said an officer controlling the onlooking crowd.

"But—"

"No special privileges."

Special privileges?

It was then Starr realized she'd instinctively grabbed her camera, with her press credentials attached to the strap. "That's not why I'm here. I just want to know if Rebecca Bradley is all right. I'm her godmother."

The officer hesitated, then turned to one side and pointed. A child stood next to an ambulance, tears rolling down her cheeks. She seemed so little and vulnerable that pain twisted inside of Starr.

No.

Becky had already lost her parents. She'd been through enough. It wasn't fair to have something else happen to her.

The policeman cleared his throat. "You can go over, but keep out of the way," he warned.

Starr spared him a single glance before threading her way toward the child. Becky's mother had been her best friend, though in the two years since Becky had been born, Starr had only seen her three times; her career as a photojournalist kept her out of the country for months on end. Horribly, she hadn't even known Amelia and Sam were dead until well after the funeral. That had been six months ago and this was the first time she'd been able to get home.

"Don't cry. Please, don't cry," begged the woman standing over Becky. "Don't worry, it's all right."

All right? Starr's honey brown eyebrows lifted. She walked to the ambulance and crouched till she was at the same height as the child. "Hey, kiddo," she murmured.

"Dr. Bradley will be furious if you take any pictures," the other woman insisted. "He doesn't like reporters."

Starr sighed and tucked her press badge into a pocket. Noah Bradley was Becky's uncle and guardian. They'd had a couple of uncomfortable telephone conversations since she'd arrived home, but she'd never met him. "You're Mrs. Dinsdale, aren't you? I'm Becky's godmother. We spoke this morning."

"Oh...Miss Granger." The woman's lined face turned pink. "I'm sorry. It's nice to meet you."

Starr gave her a brief smile, then returned her attention to Becky. "What's wrong?" she asked softly.

For a long moment the youngster gazed at her. "Kitty," she said at length, pointing to the house. "Get Kitty." Her voice held an endearing confidence that this newcomer would be able to solve the problem.

"Were you playing with Kitty?"

"They were in the playroom," the elder woman interjected. She motioned toward a second-story window and Starr looked at it thoughtfully. The fire hadn't reached that side of the building. In fact, it seemed virtually ignored by the firefighters.

"I—"

"Becky!" A moment later the child was swept into a man's arms. Compared to his generous height, Becky looked like a dainty china doll.

Starr stood and watched them, a corner of her mind appreciating the stranger's broad shoulders and clean male scent. He had Becky cuddled against his chest, and his hand stroked her gold hair with a reassuring motion.

"Don't worry, Dr. Bradley, she isn't hurt. The medics checked her over...she didn't inhale any smoke," the elder woman said quickly.

Starr's eyes widened. *This* was Noah Bradley? He was *very* different than she'd envisioned him, a complete opposite to his easygoing brother. They didn't even look alike. Sam had been blond and solid; Noah had dark brown hair and a tall, athletic body. He certainly didn't look like the grumpy, bespectacled doctor she'd envisioned from their brief discussions on the phone.

"Let her speak for herself, Mrs. Dinsdale," he said quietly. "Are you okay, Becky?"

To Starr's surprise, Becky pointed at her. "Kitty," she repeated.

Dr. Bradley gave Starr an assessing look. She couldn't tell if his impression was good or bad, and it annoyed her to realize she cared. Her life-style and career didn't lend itself to relationships...as her brief marriage had proven. Getting worked up about a man with warm, intelligent eyes wouldn't change anything.

"What about a kitty?" he asked.

"I guess it's in the house," Starr murmured.

"He's one of the neighborhood cats," Mrs. Dinsdale explained. "Becky plays with him all the time. I planned to ask you if she could take it home."

"Unca Noah, Kitty," Becky said mournfully.

"Dr. Bradley, is this lady bothering you?" queried the policeman who had talked to her earlier. "She claimed to be your niece's godmother."

Noah's eyes narrowed. He should have recognized Starr immediately—she'd become almost as famous as her photographs. "It's all right. We're...getting acquainted."

The officer nodded and faded away discretely.

"Unca Noah, Kitty!"

The emphatic tone of Becky's voice demanded his attention, and he looked at her, surprised she would talk so much in front of someone she didn't really know. Though...a lot of things about Becky surprised him. He'd quickly learned there was a huge difference between *doctoring* children and *raising* them. It was frustrating and scary...and wonderful. He'd never planned to have kids, yet Becky had crept into his aching heart. Sam was gone, but his smile and eyes were mirrored in the little girl he'd left behind.

"Let me take a look at you," he murmured, setting her on the back step of the ambulance.

An exasperated, comically adult expression crossed Becky's face. "I o'tay. Kitty."

After a brief hesitation Starr stepped back and headed for the nearest fireman. While Dr. Bradley made sure Becky was *really* okay, she'd worry about Becky's beloved kitty.

"Excuse me...?"

The official turned. "Stay back, ma'am."

She scowled at the dreaded word *ma'am*. Thirty-two wasn't old enough to be called "ma'am." "Uh...there still might be a cat in the house."

"We've already searched the building."

"But—"

"I'm sorry, but there's nothing we can do. If we find the animal, we'll bring it out." He motioned her away with his arm.

Biting back a retort, Starr gazed intently at the house. A large, spreading tree grew next to the window that supposedly belonged to the playroom. The branches were old and gnarled, and dipped low on the street side.

A definite possibility.

Starr took a deep breath and slipped around the back of the ambulance. Getting into the tree was ridiculously easy—the firemen were focused on the west side of the house. They certainly didn't have time to notice a woman climbing into the bed of an old pickup and then chinning herself onto a low limb.

It wasn't until she was high in the air that Starr realized she still carried her favorite camera around her neck and shoulder. Not that it hindered her; she'd taken her cameras into every type of dangerous situation, until they almost seemed a part of her body. Climbing a tree was nothing compared to dodging bullets in war-torn countries.

Except...Starr grimaced at the lingering soreness in her shoulder. She hadn't always managed to dodge the bullets. Her last assignment had resulted in a lengthy stay in the hospital.

Oh, well. Starr nudged open the window and peered in-side—it looked safe and normal, so she swung feetfirst into the playroom.

"Kitty?" she called, pausing to listen for anything that might be an animal. Of course, she had no idea if the feline was still inside the building—which made her present ac-tions rather foolishly quixotic.

"Kitty, Kitty...?" Starr plowed through a pile of cush-ions along the wall, calling, then waiting, then calling again. She checked the closet and caught a whiff of smoke drifting down from the attic access.

"Terrific," she muttered.

Circling the room, she shifted scattered toys and furni-ture, finally hearing a faint hiss.

"Kitty?"

Dropping to her knees, Starr peered into the shadowed space between the wall and a giant stuffed teddy bear. A pair of amber eyes glimmered from the corner.

"Okay, come here," she coaxed, reaching toward him.

The feline sent out a lightning set of claws and raked the back of her hand. The attack was accompanied by a low growl, similar to the sound of angry bees. She clenched her jaw and grabbed a second time. This time both hands were slashed, leaving beads of scarlet welling on her skin.

"Wretch," Starr hissed back at the cat. "I'm leaving, and you're leaving with me."

With her third grab Starr grasped the back of "Kitty's" neck and hauled him out, spitting and struggling.

"Stop that," she ordered, giving the feline a small shake. She held it up and glared into its almond-shaped eyes. After a long second of primal communication, the animal went limp and she stuffed it inside her jacket. Kitty promptly dug his claws into her body for balance, but Starr was be-yond caring.

There was a startled shout as she swung onto the tree branch, and from the corner of her eyes she saw Noah Bradley running across the yard. A faint smile curved her mouth. Dr. Bradley had "establishment" written all over him, but he still made her feel warm and shivery in the pit of her stomach. You could tolerate a lot from a man like that.

"Get the hell down here!"

Noah glared at the woman hanging upside down above him. If the fire and climb didn't kill her, he'd probably wring her fool neck.

"Ouch," she shrieked abruptly. "You ungrateful wretch," she cursed.

Noah blinked. Odd. She didn't seem to be talking to him, and she didn't seem to be in immediate danger of falling. Quite the contrary—she inched along the branch with the confident ease of a gymnast, her long hair waving like a golden brown banner in the breeze.

"Damnation," Walker O'Brien, the Astoria fire chief, growled at Noah's elbow. "How'd she get up there?" He motioned to one of his men, who trotted toward one of the trucks. "Are you okay, lady? We're getting a ladder."

By now she'd reached the center of the tree and she parted a swathe of leaves to look at them. "Don't bother. I can manage."

Walker harrumphed. "I should lock you up."

She leaned out farther and smiled at him winningly. "But you won't, will you?"

To Noah's disgust the fire chief chuckled and shook his head. "My God, Starr Granger. When did you get home?"

"A couple of days ago. I'm on vacation. You know, visiting my parents and stuff."

"And you couldn't stay out of trouble," the chief said with a grin.

"That's—" A muffled growl came from her midsection and she winced. "Ow. Maybe I'll take that ladder after all. My passenger is using me as a pincushion."

"Is that where the blood came from?" Walker asked.

Startled, Noah looked up. Sure enough, there were red streaks on Starr's hands. The front of her jacket squirmed and a furry head poked out above the zipper, squalling in fury.

"I rescued Becky's cat," she explained. "But he didn't appreciate the favor."

Just then the ladder arrived and Noah grasped it firmly. "I'll get her," he said.

Walker grinned and stepped aside. "You're the doctor."

"I don't need anyone's help," Starr protested. "Just shove the ladder against the branch and I'll manage fine."

Noah climbed up anyway. "Going into that house was crazy," he snarled.

"I've been accused of a lot of things. Crazy is mild compared to some of them."

"I'll just bet!"

"Besides, it wasn't that dangerous," she asserted. "The fire was clear on the other side of the house."

At the moment Noah didn't care if the fire was on the moon. Obviously Starr Granger was a daredevil risk taker. A rebel to common sense. Her vocabulary probably didn't even *include* words like *caution* and *yield.* "This is an old house," he said grimly. "It could have gone up like a tinderbox and you'd have been trapped."

"I took a calculated risk."

"Noah is right," Walker O'Brien said from below. "Fires in these old places are unpredictable."

Starr frowned. "Stay out of this, Walker."

He shrugged. "Hey, I fight fires. I'd just like to get back to fighting this one…if you don't mind."

"Coming, Miss Granger?" Noah held out his hand, trying to control a smug smile.

"I told you, I don't need any help. Why are you still here, anyway? You should have taken Becky home."

Noah's free hand clenched around the ladder. How dare she criticize the way he took care of Becky? A woman who couldn't even attend her best friend's wedding or goddaughter's christening. "One of the firemen fell. I was treating him. Any objections?"

A curious flicker of emotion flashed across her face. "I'm sorry. Is he badly injured?"

"Why do you care? Are you planning to write a story about it, or just take a couple of gory pictures?"

The blue-green of her eyes deepened with indignation. "That isn't fair. I'm a photojournalist, and a damned good one. I don't get my kicks out of seeing people hurt."

The cat hissed at that moment, as though mirroring the fury of the woman who had rescued him.

"Anyway," she continued, "I didn't want a story. I just wanted to get Becky's kitty for her."

Noah sighed, knowing he'd unconsciously taken his distrust of the news media out on Starr, probably because it was so easy to be angry with her. But that didn't change the fact she'd risked her life for a cat. *A cat!* He looked her squarely in the eye. "That animal could have taken care of itself."

"You're just mad because you didn't think of it first."

He glared.

"Besides," Starr continued, "the door was closed and the window was shut.... The poor thing was helpless."

"Helpless?"

Noah grunted. As far as he could tell from her scratches, that *poor thing* had five effective weapons on each of its paws. Even worse, he suspected the *helpless* little wretch was about to take up permanent residence in his house; those claws were going to do some serious damage to his leather upholstery. Of course, Becky's grape juice and peanut butter had already done a job on the furniture…and on everything else.

"Please don't dawdle," Walker advised from his position on the ground. "I still have work to do."

"Coming," Noah said tersely. He ought to have his head examined for talking to the woman in the first place, much less having a conversation with her on a ladder!

He grasped Starr's waist as she swung from the tree. Doing so was a mistake. She wiggled indignantly, but the movement only reminded him that she was a woman—soft and nicely rounded in all the right places. Her tight, jeans-clad bottom was intimately aligned with his chest and her hair flew like fragrant silk around his face. He drew a deep breath and caught the scent of honeysuckle on a warm afternoon—except honeysuckle had never smelled *that* good on a bush.

Stop. Noah groaned. He'd always heard that anger could be stimulating under the right circumstances. Yet he'd never quite believed it until now.

"I'm ready to climb down. You're in my way," she said in a muffled voice…squirming to make her point.

Noah gritted his teeth and tried to focus on anything but the sexy slide of her hips against his body. He only partially succeeded. So he thought about the scratches on her hands. They would have to be cleansed and disinfected, then bandaged.

Good, think like a doctor.

But his thoughts were entirely male as he descended with her…one slow rung at a time. Starr kept leaning away from the ladder, trying to protect the cat still snarling loud complaints from her jacket, which meant she came into closer contact with him. When they finally reached the ground, Noah's jaw ached from being clenched, and the rest of him didn't feel so great, either.

As they walked toward the ambulance she unbuttoned her jacket and unhooked the angry feline from her shirt. Becky caught sight of the animal and lunged forward.

"Mine." She held out her arms, and Noah knew his leather furniture was doomed. Kitty had just found a new home.

"Wait a second, kiddo." Starr knelt beside the child, holding the feline's paws firmly in her hands.

"Careful, Becky," Noah warned. "He's a little upset right now, so be gentle."

Becky leaned forward and gave Kitty a series of solid pats on his head. "O'tay," she said. A loud purr rose from the cat and his eyes closed ecstatically.

"*Now* he purrs?" Starr muttered. "Swell. Why couldn't he have done that while I was saving his life?"

"Take care of Becky for a moment," Noah said to Mrs. Dinsdale. "I need to treat Mrs. Granger's wounds."

Starr handed the cat to the baby-sitter and followed him to the rear of the ambulance, an enigmatic smile on her generous mouth.

"Let's take a look," he said, holding out his hand.

"Uh-uh. I want him to do it." Starr pointed to the emergency medical technician.

An exasperated sigh rose from Noah's chest. "I'm a very good doctor."

"I'm sure you are. But I still want him."

"Oh, for Pete's sake!"

Noah stepped back and let the EMT take over. The man efficiently dealt with the scratches, then pointed to the red stains on her shirt, visible beneath the jacket. "Is that blood from your hands?"

For the first time Starr seemed uncomfortable. "Er…no. Kitty got a little wild when I climbed out of the window. But it's okay, I'll take care of it myself." She zipped the jacket to her throat as her gaze darted sideways, colliding with Noah's. He instantly remembered the intimate contact between their bodies as they'd climbed down the ladder.

"We can step into the ambulance if you'd like," the technician suggested.

"No, I'll take care of it later."

"Cat scratches get infected easily. Perhaps you'd feel more comfortable if Dr. Bradley examined you," the EMT said smoothly.

"Uh…I don't think so," Starr murmured.

Noah lifted his hand in exasperation. Was she holding a grudge? Admittedly, he hadn't been very accommodating when she'd called, asking to take Becky for a weekend. His niece was still adjusting to her parents' deaths, and he didn't want her daily routine upset for an absentee god-mother, visiting on a whim. Maybe that explained Starr's reluctance to accept his help.

"We need to talk. Sit down," he growled, pointing to the convenient step on the vehicle.

The EMT grinned and said he'd check in with the fire chief. Neither of them watched as he slipped away.

"I'm not—"

"Down!" Noah put his hands on Starr's shoulders and pushed. She winced at the pressure, drawing the left side of her body away from him. A worried frown creased his mouth. "What's wrong?"

"Nothing."

"Tell me another whopper, okay? One I might actually believe."

Starr sighed. "It's an old injury, and none of your business. Besides, I'm fine. I don't need a doctor for a couple of scratches. It's silly.''

"I don't understand," Noah said, attempting to sound reasonable. It was quite a struggle, because he felt anything *but* reasonable. "Think of me as a physician, not a man."

Her enigmatic smile returned. "Let's get one thing perfectly clear between us—I'm *not* your patient, and you're *not* my doctor."

"Do you have something against doctors?"

"Not particularly."

Noah rubbed his forehead. Starr Granger was having an unfortunate effect on him—she made him insane. "Then what's wrong, Miss...er...Ms. Granger?" he asked carefully.

She leaned toward him. "Make it easy. Call me Starr." A complex mixture of emotion glimmered in her blue-green eyes. "There's a perfectly good reason I don't want you to be my doctor."

"Oh? What is it?"

The cool, unbandaged tips of her fingers stroked his jaw. "They say actions speak louder than words, so I'll just have to show you." Her lips brushed his mouth and the heat went clear to his toes.

"What was that supposed to prove?" he asked, his voice gritty with restraint. The last thing he'd expected from the rebellious Starr was a kiss.

"I thought it was obvious. I guess I'll have to try one more time." An instant later she flowed against him, filling his senses with warmth and the scent of honeysuckle.

Unable to resist, Noah slid his fingers into the soft silk of her hair and pulled her closer. She tasted like an exotic fruit, provocative and mysterious, with infinite layers of texture and passion.

He knew exactly what she was telling him. The American Medical Association disapproved of kisses between doctors and patients, but Starr hadn't let him become her doctor. They were just a man and woman, kissing in front of half the Astoria fire department. Somehow that didn't seem to matter.

After an endless moment she pulled away.

"See you later, Dr. Bradley," she said, spinning on her heel and walking away.

Noah's mouth dropped open as she disappeared. "I'll be damned," he muttered.

He shook his head, trying to clear her tantalizing fragrance from his senses. Starr Granger had all the physical equipment to make a man feel…restless. But he didn't want to get involved with *anyone,* much less a globe-trotting journalist who took incredible chances to get her photographs.

Not that it mattered. Starr had probably just kissed him because of excess adrenaline. He didn't consider himself boring, but he was hardly the type of man to attract a woman with her explosive life-style.

A reluctant smile curved Noah's mouth when he realized he was just making excuses. His common sense told him to forget the sensual fire in Starr's restless eyes and supple body—he just didn't want to.

Chapter Two

Noah groaned as he stared at the newspaper from the previous day. Thoroughly annoyed, he slapped his cup down on the breakfast table.

On the front page was a picture of Mrs. Dinsdale's old house, surrounded by firefighters. That wasn't the bad news. The *bad* news was the back page, where the story continued. A second article augmented the sketchy information—all about one of Astoria's more famous citizens, Starr Granger.

"Damned reporters," he muttered, the paper crumpling between his fingers.

Next to a smiling publicity shot of Starr, was a picture of both Starr and Noah in front of the ambulance...kissing. The caption beneath read "Local doctor lures prize winning photographer back home." He had his arm around Starr's waist and she was arched against him.

Great, just great. That's all he needed.

He didn't remember putting his arms around Starr. But he remembered the softness of feminine curves pressed against him, the scent of honeysuckle…the provocative flavor of her mouth. He remembered the shifting shades of blue and green in her eyes, and the affectionate way she'd looked at Becky. *Those* memories had kept him awake the night before, aching with hunger.

Starr had a terrible effect on a man. No matter how many times he resolved to stop thinking about her, she crept into his mind anyway. It wasn't so much that she was attractive; he'd known a lot of women more beautiful than Starr. But none of them had shimmered with such energy.

Leaning back in his chair, Noah rubbed his throbbing forehead, grateful it was Saturday so he didn't have to go into the office.

A year ago it wouldn't have bothered him to be caught kissing an attractive woman, but a year ago he hadn't been worried about keeping custody of his niece. Now, the last thing he needed was even the *appearance* of impropriety—Becky's maternal grandparents were the most uptight, conservative people he'd ever met. Fortunately Sam and Amelia's will had been very specific—they'd wanted Noah to raise their daughter if anything happened to them.

"You need a better security system," a voice said from behind him. "Almost anyone could break in."

"Damnation!" Noah leapt to his feet and spun around. He glared at his intruder. It was Rafe McKittrick, Becky's uncle on her mother's side of the family. "You installed the lousy system. It figures you could break in. Why the hell are you here?"

"I'm not staying. I have business down the coast."

"That's a relief."

The corner of Rafe's mouth lifted slightly under his mustache, which was the closest Noah had ever come to seeing him smile. "Is Becky awake?"

"No." Noah felt a faint niggle of guilt about being so

curt, but he didn't like *any* of the McKittricks, including Rafe.

The other man just nodded and tossed him the newspaper he was carrying, folded around the infamous picture. "My parents are a little upset about this, I thought you should know."

Noah made an impatient gesture. "It's not like we were sneaking out of some seedy motel. Besides, Starr is a Pulitzer Prize winner. They should love her for that, if nothing else."

Rafe shrugged noncommittally. "About Becky... Have you considered getting married so she'd have a mother?"

"What?"

"You know, married. The 'I do' routine with gold rings. I don't hold by it personally, but it would go a long way toward smoothing things with the folks. One of their biggest gripes is because you're a bachelor."

"Wrong," Noah retorted. "One of their biggest gripes is that Sam and I were raised by a single father who drank himself into an early grave. We never had the right highbrow background to suit them. As for me being a bachelor...I'll get married to please myself, and no one else."

"Suit yourself."

For a long while after Rafe left, Noah stared into space, his coffee growing cold. He didn't think the McKittricks could take Becky away from him—they'd have to prove he was unfit. Yet he couldn't help worrying. They were powerful people, with powerful friends. And they used the newspapers they owned to pillory anyone they didn't like.

That isn't fair.

Noah shifted, almost believing he could hear Starr Granger's voice echoing in his mind. Intellectually, he knew she was different than the nosy, truth-twisting reporters he'd dealt with since Sam's death—the reporters

who had suggested Sam was responsible for the fatal crash
of the twin engine Cessna, either by pilot incompetence or
impaired judgment. Yet it was hard to separate her from
the McKittricks.

With bleak eyes, Noah gazed out at the view. The back
of the house overlooked the turbulent beauty of the Pacific
Ocean, and visible to the far right was the broad opening
of the Columbia River. A nice view for a nice house; a
fine, healthy home for a child. Except "nice" and
"healthy" weren't enough to satisfy the McKittricks. They
didn't like anyone who didn't fit their mold of acceptance.

A small weight, imbued with warmth, leaned against his
leg. Becky—tousle-haired and yawning—in her sleepers.
Without a word she crawled into his lap and settled against
his chest.

Noah's heart flip-flopped.

He smoothed damp tendrils of hair away from her face.
Playing the indulgent uncle had been easy—learning to be
a father was far more difficult. Truthfully, sometimes it was
easier when Becky was asleep. Wide-awake, she was a
complete mystery to him. She smeared bananas on his suits
and fed oatmeal to the compact disc player. She didn't talk
very much so he couldn't tell what she was thinking. She
said "no" with alarming regularity.

But it would kill him to lose her.

The thought stayed with Noah as he dressed Becky for
the day. He was still awkward with the morning routine of
caring for a child, and her bedroom usually resembled a
disaster area by the time they were finished. He hadn't expected a daily fashion dilemma with a two-year-old, but
Becky was fussier than any New York model.

Today was no exception.

She didn't want to wear the Cinderella outfit; she wanted
the one with kitty cats. Only, when he found the kitty-cat

sweater, she'd changed her mind and wanted something else. Since she didn't communicate well, he ended up holding garments up one by one, trying to figure out which one she really wanted. Of course, she ended up deciding to wear the Cinderella dress after most of the closet and her dresser drawers were empty.

As they headed back to the kitchen—finally dressed—Noah sighed. When it came to Becky, his extensive medical education flew out the window. All the child-rearing theories in the world didn't amount to a hill of beans when confronted by an obstinate two-year-old.

Patience. He just needed patience.

Becky's tantrums were probably caused by the upheaval in her life. And no wonder. Losing Sam and Amelia had been hard for both of them.

Noah was contemplating the next battle, what to fix for breakfast, when the phone rang. "Hello?"

"You sound breathless." Starr's melodic voice sent an unusual reaction through Noah's gut. "How is Becky doing? Any problems because of the excitement?"

"Er…Ms. Granger. No, she's fine."

"I thought you were going to call me Starr."

"I wasn't going to call you at all," he said bluntly. No matter how attractive, he didn't plan on spending time with Starr Granger. She was too…volatile. Too unpredictable. Too *everything*.

She laughed, seeming unperturbed by his rudeness. "I'd like to see Becky. We didn't have much chance for a visit with everything that happened."

"Uh-huh," he murmured.

"How about this afternoon?"

Noah shifted uncomfortably. "I think next week would be better."

There was a long pause. "I won't be in town for very

long. I'm on vacation, but I have to go back to work eventually.''

"I didn't realize you took vacations.''

"What is that supposed to mean?'' Starr asked, a faintly indignant huff in her voice.

"Nothing. Except…well…why the sudden interest in Becky? Hell, you didn't even show up at her baptism— they had to get someone to stand in for you.''

Starr sighed. "We discussed this when I called the first time. I was on assignment. I explained to Amelia and Sam—they understood.''

Noah gritted his teeth. Fine. Maybe Amelia and Sam had understood, but *he* didn't. "This is just one of your impulsive whims,'' he growled. "Like kissing me in front of everyone. Have you seen yesterday's paper?''

Starr laughed. "I thought you'd be unhappy about that.''

"Unhappy?" he said loudly. "The McKittricks live only a hundred miles away and they watch everything I do. Hell—they're probably filing for custody right now.''

"You're just overreacting. They aren't that bad, you know.''

"Oh, sure!''

"Unca Noah?'' A hand tugged on his trousers. Distracted, he looked down at Becky's worried face.

"It's all right, baby,'' he reassured. "Go play with your toys…or with Kitty.''

"Not baby,'' she informed him. Her bottom lip pouted out and he winced. When she had a tantrum she *really* had a tantrum. For all her sweetness, his niece was as stubborn as a mule.

"Noah…Dr. Bradley, are you there?''

"Just a minute, Ms. Granger.'' He leaned down to Becky and tweaked one of her braids. It wasn't a very good braid, but the best he'd been able to manage with her silky fine hair. "That's right, you're not a baby," he agreed. "Breakfast will be ready in a few minutes. Can you wait a while?"

After a long pause she nodded and trotted to the corner, where Kitty was flicking his tail and observing his food bowl. Becky thumped his back and he turned and rubbed himself against her so hard, she toppled onto her bottom with a giggle.

Noah shook his head. Kitty was unaccountably gentle with Becky. He straightened and tucked the receiver under his chin. "Starr?"

"Yes."

"We'll have to talk about what's best for Becky. When may I see you?"

"Anytime, I guess. I'll be here the rest of the day. I'm staying with my mother and father. They have a store called From Earth and Sky—they live in the back."

"Good. Becky is supposed to spend the morning with some friends, so I'll get her settled before coming over." Noah scribbled the directions and hung up with a terse goodbye.

Maybe, just maybe, under different circumstances he'd enjoy knowing Starr Granger. But maybe not. Sam's death had reminded him how fragile life could be. He didn't want to care about someone who treated it so casually.

Even a woman as intriguing as Starr.

Two hours later Noah parked his car and stared at the directions Starr had given him, then back at the house. A health food store? Starr's parents owned a *health food store*.

He'd expected something entirely different. An art gallery perhaps. A snobbish, upscale gallery. The kind of straitlaced, conservative place the McKittricks would patronize. But it wasn't, so how had Starr Granger and Amelia McKittrick ever become friends?

A sensation of unreality crept over him as he stepped through the gate and watched a pair of brown rabbits hop away, disappearing into the lush wilderness of the garden. It was like something from one of Becky's storybooks—a combination of *Peter Cottontail* and *Alice in Wonderland.* Baskets of flowers and herbs hung from the overhanging eaves. Moss grew in velvet swathes between flagstones on the path and at the foundation of the house. And on the porch a mama cat lounged in the sun, three kittens busily nursing.

Warily he opened the front door and saw a plant-filled interior. Light cascaded through a myriad of crystals, sending fractured rainbows dancing through the air and across various wares in jars and bins. A woman sat at a loom under the far window, examining the pattern she was weaving. After a moment she looked up and smiled.

"Welcome," she said softly.

"Uh...er...thanks," Noah stuttered. Plainly this was Starr's mother. They had the same stunning cheekbones, the same clear blue-green eyes, the same rich, golden brown hair. But where Starr radiated saucy self-reliance, her mother had the sweet, untroubled innocence of a child.

She rose to her feet, looking oddly sophisticated in a natural-weave skirt and sweater. "Would you like some tea? I have some wonderful chamomile I grew myself." She paused and studied him for a moment. "Or would you prefer peppermint and honey?"

"Er...no...nothing, thanks," Noah said quickly, unable to repress a small shudder.

"I understand. You're a friend of my daughter's."

He blinked. Psychic? "Well...sort of."

Just then a man strolled through a door in the rear.

"Have you seen the radish seeds, Moon Bright? I want to start some sprouts for salad."

"Blue," she admonished gently. "You know Morning Star doesn't like sprouts."

"But these are different." Blue looked at Noah, whose jaw had dropped at the vivid collection of names. "You must be here to see Morning Star."

"Morning Star?" he repeated.

"She prefers to be called Starr," Moon Bright explained.

Noah rubbed his temple. What...did he have a tattoo on his forehead? A warning sign? Danger. This Man Has Encountered Starr Granger. His Life Will Never Be The Same.

"Er...how did you know?"

"The suit," Blue said.

"No herbal tea," Moon Bright added. She sighed. "None of her friends like herbal tea. Oh, dear, you're not that man she married, are you?"

Married? Noah's eyes narrowed as he realized how little he knew about Starr. And the worse part was learning she'd given him insomnia when she was definitely unavailable. He didn't agree with "open" marriages.

"No," he said shortly. "I'm not the one she married."

Moon Bright appeared relieved. "I'm so glad."

Noah couldn't decide if he himself was insulted, or relieved. Marriage to Starr Granger would surely lead a man to stark raving insanity.

"Dad, where are your sales receipts for the past quarter?" exclaimed the "wife" in question as she swept into the room. In contrast to the artless tranquillity of her parents, she was a whirlwind of energy. "I can't do an income projection without them."

"You have company, dear."

When Starr recognized Noah, her eyes widened. "Oh...Dr. Bradley. You're earlier than I expected."

"A doctor?" Moon Bright shook her head sadly. "Darling, I think we should talk."

"Not now, mother." Distracted, she looked at her father as he lifted various containers from the shelves and inspected the contents. "Dad, what are you looking for?"

"Radish seeds, dear. They make a very tangy sprout. I'm sure you'll like them."

Starr rubbed the back of her neck as though in sudden, acute pain.

"I'm glad he's not the one you married," Moon Bright murmured. "At least he said he wasn't."

"Uh…" Starr glanced briefly in Noah's direction.

He glared, deciding he was both relieved *and* insulted. "Please, tell us about the man you *did* marry, since I'm not the 'one.'"

"There's not much to tell. I'm divorced."

"You and Chase would still be together if you hadn't stifled yourselves with legal boundaries. It's so unnatural. Remember that next time, dear," her mother advised. She looked at Noah and shook her head again, clearly alarmed he might be "the next time."

"Thanks, Mom. I think I'll go for a walk. I need some air. Try to find those sales receipts while I'm gone, okay, Dad?" She grabbed Noah's arm and propelled him through the door. He endured the fast-paced march for two full blocks down the hillside before slowing her into a more normal pace.

Normal? Hell, he doubted anything was normal around Starr. Noah whistled beneath his breath. "Morning Star" hadn't rebelled from a straitlaced home, she'd escaped herbal tea and radish sprout salads. Compared to her parents, she was a conservative rule follower, a staid pillar of the community. The difference was phenomenal.

"Let's clarify something," he said speculatively. "Your real name is Morning Star?"

"My passport says Starr Granger."

"What does your birth certificate say?"

Starr grimaced in resignation. "Go ahead and laugh, get it out of your system. My mother is Moon Bright, and my father is Blue River. Of course, those aren't their original names, just the ones they picked in their search for self-expression."

"Moon Bright and Blue River are self-expressive?" he asked, incredulous.

She shrugged. "Don't knock it. My mother originally wanted to be called Aurora Borealis."

"I…uh…can see that would be awkward."

"It was too much of a mouthful, even for my father," Starr agreed. "They kind of evolved into relaxed 'New Agers.' You know, crystals and nonconventional spiritualism…that kind of thing. They were disappointed when I preferred a different life-style."

"You can say that again. Jeez, you even got married. What a terrible blow that must have been. Don't you know that marriage is the primary cause of divorce?"

She gave him a dirty look, equaling the one *he'd* given her not long before. "What do you want, Dr. Bradley?"

He clucked at her. "I'm not your doctor. You made sure of that, didn't you?"

Starr was beginning to regret ever setting eyes on Noah Bradley. But she couldn't regret kissing him, not completely. If she'd felt a tenth of the sizzle kissing her ex-husband as she'd felt kissing Noah, her marriage would have lasted a lot longer. Of course, she and Chase had never been together long enough in the same place to make *anything* last…including sizzle.

"I'm impulsive. You said so yourself," Starr felt obliged

to point out, though she didn't expect *Dr.* Bradley to understand. She did plenty of rash things she later regretted. On the other hand, she'd bet Noah always had good, solid reasons for his actions. He was that kind of man.

"I think calling you impulsive is too mild," Noah drawled. "Running into a burning house goes way beyond impulsive."

"I didn't run, I climbed. And it was perfectly safe. By the way, how *is* Kitty?"

"Kitty didn't actually belong to us, but he's been adopted. In less than twenty-four hours he's ruined a silk tie, eaten a salmon fillet without permission and climbed the living room drapes." Noah looked heavenward as though asking for divine intervention. "When I tried to get him down he catapulted off my shoulder and landed in the aquarium. Unfortunately, the top was off."

A choking sound escaped from Starr's throat.

He frowned. "It isn't funny. I nearly lost my ear in the process."

"I'll bet the fish didn't like it, either." Starr laughed as she envisioned Noah Bradley in a battle of wills with "Kitty." Boy, she wished she'd been there. It would have been priceless.

"Now that Kitty is fully aware of the aquarium, he's spent hours in front of it, batting at the fish," Noah concluded gloomily. "That animal splashed water and fish for ten feet, then made mincemeat out of me when I tried to rescue him."

"I know," Starr said, with somewhat less humor than before. She flexed her hands, which still bore the marks of Kitty's first "rescue." His nine lives were being rapidly depleted.

"Let me see how you're healing," Noah offered.

"Uh...I..." She stuttered to a halt. Her feelings toward

Dr. Bradley were a peculiar mixture of curiosity and screeching alarm. "I thought you were angry at me," she said quickly. "Because of the picture…and everything."

"I am." For an instant his expression turned somber. "But I'd hate for you to get an infection."

Starr swallowed, contemplating the dangers of getting close to Noah Bradley. He was obviously an upstanding member of the establishment, yet the dark heat in his eyes tugged at her, coaxing an elemental response. No man— including her ex-husband—had ever made her feel that way.

Until now.

And that made him dangerous. *How* dangerous Starr didn't want to find out. She'd learned the hard way that attraction didn't last, and that ten seconds of fleeting pleasure wasn't worth messing up the bed.

"Starr?"

"Okay, but you're still not my doctor," she said hastily. *Foolishly.* Becoming his patient would have been an easy way to protect herself from…*him.* "We're just comparing battle scars, understand?"

His slow, reluctant smile spoke volumes, including a reminder of the kiss they'd shared. Well, hell. Even though nothing would come of it, how could he say being impulsive was so bad?

"If this is 'show and tell,' there are a few other places I wouldn't mind seeing," he suggested.

To Starr's astonishment, she had to struggle to keep from turning red. Lord, she hadn't blushed since she was a teenager, and never to such an obvious gambit. But then, Noah Bradley was *no* teenager, and a far cry from the tough newsmen she usually encountered.

"Here," she said, holding her hands out in front of her. Noah took them and examined the healing wounds. His fingers were strong and hard, yet sensitive enough to catch the quickening rush of her pulse. "Pretty good," he murmured. "No signs of infection. What about the scratches on your shoulder?"

"I'm hardly going to show you *them*, am I?" Starr asked, trying to free her hands.

Crisp, salt-laden air blew inward from the ocean, unaffected by the sunshine. Even so, Starr could feel the warmth from Noah's body. He'd be pleasant to snuggle up with on a cold night—much better than an electric blanket.

Jeez. Get a grip.

Her nose wrinkled as she scolded herself. It had to be the inactivity. She was always busy, always moving. She might work in the wilds of Africa for months at a time, then spend the next fourteen weeks rushing from airplane to airplane. Whenever her frantic life-style got stale, she came home to Astoria; a few days with her parents were guaranteed to give her wanderlust again.

But was that what she really wanted? To keep racing around the world, without belonging anywhere? Lately she'd been feeling a growing restlessness, though she didn't quite understand *why*.

Starr shivered, but more from uncertainty than from cold. A moment later Noah shrugged his coat off and dropped it around her shoulders. It was a chivalrous thing to do, the kind of act he probably did without thinking.

Where did men like that come from? Or, she decided, where had men like that gone *to?* He certainly wasn't like any of the hard-nosed professionals she'd encountered in her travels. She'd dealt with them all—environmentalists, poachers, State Department officials, even a tough old naturalist who hadn't wanted to share his lions with her until he'd discovered her affinity with felines.

Noah was different. Chivalrous and old-fashioned.

Though…the sensual way he watched her was anything *but* old-fashioned.

"What are you thinking?" he asked quietly.

She shook her head. "Nothing. That is…I've been wondering. That kitchen fire in Mrs. Dinsdale's house put her out of commission for a while—I understand she's gone to visit her sister during the cleanup. Maybe you'd consider letting me take Becky for a weekend, or maybe even a week or two. My parents have lots of room and they love children."

Abruptly Noah stepped back, a remote expression on his face. "That's nice of you, but I still don't think it's a good idea. Becky needs routine and stability."

Starr curled her fingers in loose fists. She knew it was important for a child to have routine. Hadn't she always wished for normal parents herself? Yet she didn't think Noah's motives were entirely innocent.

"Anyway," he said, "you're out of the country a lot. It might not be good for Becky to get too attached to you. I think it would be best for everyone if you limited your visits to casual contact."

"Casual?" Starr narrowed her eyes. "Amelia was my best friend. She wanted me to be her daughter's godmother. I don't think 'casual' is what she had in mind."

"If you cared about Amelia, you would have come home more often," Noah muttered.

"I *did* care. Amelia was like a sister to me."

"Really?" Bitterness edged his voice.

Starr could almost hear the "but" hanging in the air. *But*…if she'd cared so much, she would have at least attended her best friend's funeral. She smiled tightly. "You know, it's a shame we didn't meet a long time ago. We could have gotten a head start on hating each other."

For an astonished moment Noah stared at her, then he

laughed. "You're something else. I'll bet your mouth got you into plenty of trouble when you were a kid."

"Constantly. But never at home—Mom and Dad just considered it a form of self-expression. They're big on self-expression."

"Having met your parents, I can believe it. How did you ever get to know the McKittricks? I doubt they're health food fanatics."

She shrugged. "It's a long story, but they became friends in college. Look, I may not be ideal mother material, but I want to have a part in Becky's life."

As soon as the words left Starr's mouth, the stubbornly feminine part of her cringed...the part that wanted Noah Bradley to see her as a woman. On the other hand, she was being honest. Children had never figured into her plans for the future. She was taking an interest in Becky because she'd made a promise to Amelia.

He gave her an exasperated look. "Great. You ignored my niece for over two years, now you want to see her. After a while you'll lose interest and go back to your life."

For a long minute she was speechless. "I didn't ignore her. I sent gifts and visited whenever I came home."

"Which was practically never."

"I have a job to do."

"I know. And isn't it great—they'll never run out of wars and disasters for you to photograph!"

"You...you..." For a moment Starr's smart mouth failed her. She wanted to hit him. She wanted to smack that scornful expression right off his handsome face.

But since violence was out, she said a Kurdish swear-word she'd learned in her travels, wiggled from the confining folds of his jacket and threw it over a convenient rose-bush.

"Go to hell," she snapped and stormed away.

Chapter Three

"Wait a minute!" A stunned Noah yanked his jacket from the rosebush and heard the fabric rip.

Terrific.

He had all the tact of a rhinoceros. What else could he do to screw things up?

"Starr, please wait." He caught up in front of her parents' health food store and grabbed her arm. She spun around in time for him to see pain temporarily replace the anger in her face.

"What's wrong?"

"I'm fine." Nevertheless, she put her hand on her left shoulder and rubbed. "It's just the scratches."

Noah sighed. He didn't believe her, yet he couldn't force her to explain. "Look, I'm sorry I got carried away...I don't like reporters."

"Gee, that's a surprise. I wouldn't have guessed."

He sighed. Ever since Sam had died, he'd been fighting with the McKittricks. Unfortunately, since Starr was both a friend of the McKittricks and Becky's godmother, that put her directly in the middle of the battle. "You weren't in the country when Sam and Amelia were killed, so you don't know what it was like."

She nodded warily. "I was out of touch. I haven't even had a chance to talk to Rafe. He called this morning, but I was taking a walk."

"Well…there was a lot of publicity after the accident. The McKittricks are influential because of that chain of newspapers they own—not to mention being friends with everyone who *is* anyone in Oregon, including the present governor."

"What does that have to do with it?"

"Everything." Noah massaged the back of his neck. "They never liked Sam. They thought he was presumptuous to marry their daughter. Amelia must have told you how much they disliked him."

"They didn't dislike him," she murmured. "Not exactly."

"Really?"

"Okay, I guess they would have preferred her marrying someone else," Starr admitted, wrinkling her nose. "Deep down they're nice people."

Noah decided the "deep down" part must be *way* deep down—like in the Marianas Trench. He took a breath, knowing it might be foolish to confide in Starr, yet also knowing his sister-in-law and brother had trusted her. "The McKittricks blame Sam for the accident. The way they see things, if he hadn't married their daughter, she wouldn't have been in that plane with him," he said, bitterness tinging his voice.

Starr's eyes widened. "I'm sorry. That isn't fair," she whispered.

Turning, Noah stared down at the town. Below them the Columbia River flowed to meet the ocean, a glistening silver ribbon across the western horizon. The ocean was constant, unchanging. He needed something that couldn't change, something that couldn't be ripped away with a single phone call. *Like Sam.*

He sensed compassion in Starr's gaze, yet he couldn't handle any more sympathy. Everybody was sorry about his brother. His friends, his co-workers, even the checker at the supermarket. Everybody "understood." How could they understand? He'd lost the person he loved most in the world, the only family he had left except for Becky. He couldn't endure losing anyone else.

"They aren't too happy with me, either," he added harshly. "Maybe it would be different if I was a wealthy, big-city specialist. But I'm not. I'm just a general practitioner who doesn't play golf, and doesn't plan on getting filthy rich."

"There's nothing wrong with that."

"Thanks. But you'll never convince the McKittricks I'm a proper guardian."

Starr winced. Amelia had been raised mostly by nannies and servants—she'd wanted a different childhood for Becky. The elder McKittricks were decent in a stuffy kind of way, but they'd been lousy parents.

"All right." She crossed her arms over her chest and looked at him squarely. "They never liked Sam, they don't approve of you and they own a bunch of newspapers. What has that got to do with hating the news media?"

He snorted. "You have no idea what it was like—newspaper articles implying Sam was at fault, suggesting pilot error." Noah threw out his hand angrily. "There wasn't any error, Sam was a great pilot. Then after Becky was put in my custody, the reporters started hounding me again, questioning my fitness and harassing me about my relationship with the McKittricks."

"Oh."

That was all she said. A single word.

"You see, don't you?" he appealed. "It was like being surrounded by sharks."

"I'm a photojournalist," Starr said quietly. "Not that kind of reporter. And I've spent most of my career taking nature photos, which is completely different."

Noah hesitated, remembering his thoughts earlier that morning. Starr was a respected photographer. She wouldn't agree with the McKittricks' muckraking tactics, no matter how close their friendship might be.

Oh, hell. He'd been a jerk. He'd let his temper override his common sense. "I...uh...I'm sorry."

"Never mind." She shrugged and hooked her thumbs into the belt loops of her jeans. Noah groaned silently, because the motion reminded him how great she looked in those skin-fitting denims.

So much for a guilty conscience.

It would have been nice to talk to his brother about Starr, to get his opinion. God, he missed that...missed talking and laughing with someone who knew him better than anyone else in the world. He would have told Sam about Starr's tight jeans and her tight bottom. Then he'd have complained about his lack of self-control and latent immaturity. The big goon would have sniggered and called him a Neanderthal—marriage had turned Sam into a real nineties kind of guy.

Noah gave himself a mental slap. He'd progressed beyond the ogling stage in his early twenties. Hadn't he? Maybe it was just Starr. She was entirely too intriguing. And at the moment, she was also entirely too accessible.

He opened his mouth. "Do you know how tight your jeans are?"

"What?" She let her hands drop.

Uh-oh. A classic Freudian slip of the tongue. "I just meant...er...they look great."

Watching closely, Noah could have sworn a trace of color touched her cheeks. Of course, it might have been from the crisp ocean breeze; Starr wasn't the blushing type.

"You're a Neanderthal," she said tartly.

Suddenly Noah felt a lot better. Granted, it wasn't Sam insulting him, but it was the same insult. Maybe they could just be friends.

No... He stopped and looked her up and down again. Friends *and* lovers maybe, but never just friends. A platonic relationship with Starr would never work. *Never.*

"How do you work in those? I mean, they're really tight," he said, a smile tugging at his lips. "I'm surprised you can even walk."

Starr ran her fingers over her thighs, enjoying the feel of the soft, worn fabric. She didn't think jeans were worth anything until they'd been washed and worn to the last inch of their life. "Not that my clothes are any concern of yours, but I have big, baggy ones when I'm working, with lots of room in the pockets."

"That's good, because there's no room in *those* pockets. Thank God," he said with an exaggerated leer.

"Men," she mumbled. They were all the same, no matter what language they spoke. Still, it was kind of cute. And rather surprising, considering the man was wearing a suit. *On a Saturday,* no less. It made him seem like a regular guy, not an uptight yuppie.

Uptight?

Starr bit her lip to keep from laughing. This whole thing was awfully funny, because Noah reminded her of the McKittricks, who were also a bit uptight.

Except...on him it was okay.

All at once panic hit Starr. She didn't want to care about

Noah Bradley. She didn't want to think he was cute, or any other superlative like handsome or sexy, or even likable. And she certainly didn't want to fall in love with him. So why had she kissed him? Temporary insanity?

Get a grip, she ordered silently. Her response to Noah was way out of proportion. Like getting so upset at his negative attitude toward reporters. She was used to that—she shouldn't have let it become personal.

Noah lifted one of her hands and traced lazy circles over the base of her wrist.

Drat.

Starr tried to control her feminine response to his touch...and failed utterly. It was baffling. How could he make her so hot and shaky with a single touch?

"What are you doing?" she asked, a shade of desperation creeping into her tone as his gaze dropped, taking in the taut thrust of her breasts.

"Damned if I know," he muttered. "I must be losing my mind. What is it about you that keeps me so confused?"

Starr couldn't be sure, but she suspected his confusion was caused by his intellect arguing with male instinct. On a purely rational level he obviously didn't want to get involved with her. But on a physical level...maybe he wasn't so sure. A small, embarrassed smile tugged at her lips—it was flattering, even though she didn't want to get involved, either.

Of course, for men, sex didn't necessarily mean "getting involved." *Hmmm.* She'd have to think about that for a while. And what was so wrong with her anyway?

"For the record..." she said thoughtfully, "what do you dislike so much about me? I mean, aside from my impulsiveness and career. Oh, yes—and the fact I'm a friend of the McKittricks."

"You want some kind of list?" he asked, giving her a teasing grin.

She smiled back—showing her teeth—and Noah's expression became a lot more cautious. "Just hit the high points," she said with an overdose of sweetness.

"Er...I don't dislike you. But we've got different lives. Different priorities."

"And?"

"And nothing."

"Aren't you going to pull Becky into this? You seem determined to dictate the terms of my relationship with her."

He sighed, an *I'm being as patient as possible* sigh. "I just suggested you keep things casual, at least until she's a little older. She's too young to really understand what happened to her mother and father, and she's having a few problems adjusting. I don't want anything else to upset her. She could get really fond of you, and then..." He shrugged.

Starr blinked. She respected Noah's protectiveness of Becky, though it seemed to be a little in the *over*protective category. Yet she couldn't help thinking he was mostly looking for an excuse, not so much to keep her out of his niece's life, but out of *his*. "I'd never do anything to hurt her."

"Not intentionally."

"Look, if you're talking about the fire again, I was perfectly safe."

"Yes," he said tensely. "I'm talking about the fire. I'm talking about something happening to you...something permanent. You do some pretty crazy things."

Starr glared. "What do you mean by that?"

Uh-oh. Rocky territory. Noah already knew the warning signs. Flashing eyes. A stiffened spine. And a tightness to her generous mouth worthy of a schoolmarm. Sheesh, she

was prickly. One innocent little statement and she was
ready to flatten him.

"Hell, Starr. Look at your life. You don't exactly live
by the rules."

"Your rules, maybe."

"Dammit. You're deliberately misunderstanding me!"
Noah waited a tense minute, not wanting to say something
he'd regret. Starr's life was her own concern. If she wanted
to throw it away for some photographs, then he didn't have
the right to object. But he wanted to. He wanted to nail her
shoes to the floor so she couldn't take such wild chances.
"You have an unusual life-style. Most people are a little
more…"

"Responsible?" Her tone could have cut glass. "I've
been responsible all my life. Somebody had to be. My parents were too busy hanging crystals and exploring their
'auras' to do things like pay bills and file their taxes."

Startled, Noah looked at Starr, remembering the calm
tranquillity of Blue River and Moon Bright. Nice people,
but not equipped to deal with the world. Starr must have
taken care of them, even as a child. Responsible? She was
probably sick to death of responsibility.

"I didn't mean to suggest you weren't responsible," he
said warily. "But you take a lot of risks in your work."
There, he'd said it very diplomatically.

"I'm very careful," she sputtered. "I was in a safe zone,
so it should have been all right. I only got shot because the
fighting shifted unexpectedly."

He froze. "Shot? When did you get shot?"

"Uh…" Starr paused. "A while back, but it wasn't a
big deal. I thought that's what you meant about taking
risks."

Noah wished he'd never started the conversation. He'd
treated gunshot wounds during his residency at an inner-

city trauma center. Bullets did nasty things to healthy bodies. He tried to remember any news reports about her getting injured, but nothing came to mind. And with a woman like Starr, ignorance was bliss—not that his personal feelings were involved. It just offended his professional sensibilities for her to be so reckless with her life.

Sure. Personal feelings had nothing to do with his reaction to Starr. Right. You bet.

"Let's forget it," he said finally.

"Fine."

Reaching out his hand, he couldn't keep from drawing his finger down the curve of her cheek. "I'm sorry I upset you."

Starr blinked, then closed her eyes, afraid she'd reveal her pleasure in the gentle caress. However irritating, Noah was a tremendously sensual man; a man who made her feel like a woman. He moved his hand again, sliding it into her hair and rubbing her scalp soothingly. Except it wasn't soothing; it felt erotic. Like when she'd kissed him.

Nothing could come of it, though. While she had enjoyed the petting and closeness of sex with her husband, there hadn't been any fireworks. Somehow she'd always suspected *she* was the one who lacked sizzle, not Chase.

Very depressing.

Not an experience she cared to repeat.

Yet it felt so good, having Noah close to her, touching her. He could make her reconsider this sizzle business.

Watch out, her defenses warned. But the voice was sluggish, like it had been smothered a few too many times.

Starr moaned. She was doing it again…forgetting common sense. On the other hand, common sense wasn't any comfort on a lonely night—and lately the nights had been especially lonely.

"What are you trying to charm me out of?" she muttered, opening her eyes and giving a warning glance.

"Is that what you think I'm doing, charming you?" Noah smiled his impossible smile and she frowned.

"You're trying, anyway."

The devilish gleam in his face deepened. "I'd kiss you, but I think your mother is spying on us through the window."

"Don't be ridiculous. She'd never do anything so cosmically conventional." She looked around nevertheless.

"Wanna bet?"

"I never bet on certainties."

"Okay, maybe it was your father. But those curtains were swaying over something." Seeming almost absent-minded, Noah curled a lock of her hair around one of his fingers.

"You have a hyperactive imagination."

"No. But I feel like a teenager again." He drew nearer as his finger crept up the length of her hair.

Sighing, Starr put her hand over his and tried to liberate herself. He kept doing that—getting close, touching her in seemingly innocent ways. Why couldn't he keep his distance?

It's your own fault.

Well, of course it was her fault. She was the one who'd kissed him in the first place. That didn't mean he could keep touching her now, did it?

"You don't like me, remember?" she said when he'd gotten her really, *really* close and his hand was once again cupping the back of her head. "All that stuff about taking risks, and such."

"It's all right, you don't have to be afraid," Noah murmured. He brushed his lips across her forehead.

"I'm not afraid of you."

"Of course, Starr," he said agreeably, which annoyed her.

"If there's anything I hate, it's arrogant men."

"It's not a problem then, since I'm not arrogant."

"Ugh. What do you want?"

Noah tipped her face back. "I want to apologize properly. And...I want to know if you taste as good as I remember."

Her heart stopped beating for a second, then went into triple time. *No.* She didn't want him to kiss her. One impulsive mistake was enough. She was happy with her life and didn't want to be reminded that other possibilities existed.

"Noah, let's be practical. We don't agree on anything. We're complete opposites."

"I know." His breath fanned lightly across her lips.

She wiggled, but he didn't release her. Then she stopped wiggling, because she could feel a very male part of him responding. "Er...Noah?"

For an endless moment he stared into her eyes. "Damn," he muttered, an instant before his head lowered.

He kissed her, a fierce, hungry kiss that drove every other thought from her head. Her neck arched against the pressure of his mouth and his arms held her captive in a hard, gentle prison. A moan began deep in her throat and vanished into the fiery, seamless mating of their mouths.

Surrendering completely, Starr slid her arms about Noah's waist and held on as he devoured her—tasting her, filling her, turning her inside out. Her breasts tightened, aching with an unfamiliar need. She had never felt like this—hot and steamy and strangely safe. Noah was creating the storm, yet there he was, solid and secure in the center, the one sure harbor.

She thought—distantly—that he had an awful lot of muscles for a doctor. Like his hands, his body was fit and strong, with a controlled power. One thing was sure, when Noah Bradley kissed, he put his heart and soul into the matter. What would it be like to be loved like that? Not just physically, but emotionally…loved with a single-minded passion that didn't let anything get in the way.

A tinge of alarm sliced across Starr's concentration. She couldn't start spinning foolish dreams. Noah might find her desirable, but it wouldn't last. Rationally he didn't want to have anything to do with her. Besides, it was embarrassing to melt into a feminine puddle just because of a kiss. Right? It was just hormones, and hormones could be controlled. She had it on good authority that sex was not an essential ingredient of life.

Oh, yeah? her hormones jeered.

Okay, so she might be wrong about it. Noah could put doubts in any woman's head.

Quietly he shuddered against her, then his arms dropped away. "Starr?"

"That was…uh…"

"I know."

She put her hand against his chest, her head spinning. "We're on a public street."

"I realize that. But it didn't bother you before. The next time will be private, I promise," Noah assured grimly. He drew his thumb across the damp fullness of her mouth, his expression a troubled mix of anger and passion. Clearly he didn't entirely approve of what had happened between them, and just as clearly he believed it would happen again.

Starr frowned. Noah had been under a lot of stress; he probably wasn't thinking straight. Under different circumstances he wouldn't have looked at her twice. All at once two strong fingers lifted her chin and she realized she'd been staring at Noah's tie; it was a very nice silk tie, stylish without being outrageous. "Yes?"

"What are you thinking?"

She flicked her dry lips with the tip of her tongue, stopping when she saw his eyes darken. "I can't believe I just kissed a man who wears suits on Saturdays," she said quickly. "You're *establishment*, Noah Bradley, squared and tripled."

"At least I'm not an ax murderer...though from the way your parents acted, I'm not sure which they would have preferred. Is it just me, or all doctors?"

"Mostly doctors who associate with their daughter, but they do believe in natural healing." She stepped back and crossed her arms over her stomach, gazing at him steadily. "Now, when may I visit Becky?"

Noah sighed. "All right. Dinner tonight at my house. I'll pick you up at five."

"No," she said hastily, "I'll drive myself."

"Want an easy escape? Who worries you—Becky or me, Mr. Establishment?"

She raised one eyebrow. "I'm not worried about either of you. Becky is a sweetheart. And if I can handle a pride of African lions, I can handle you."

"That sounds interesting. I can hardly wait." He took a business card from his wallet and wrote his address on the back. "Here's where I live...it's outside of Astoria on the coast. Bring a swimsuit."

"Wait a minute." Starr chased after him as he strode to his car. "What do I need a swimsuit for?"

"For the hot tub."

"Noah Bradley, I'm not sleeping with you."

"I know." He nodded as he slid into the car and fastened his seat belt.

"I mean that," she warned, tapping the roof of the car

for emphasis, the card clutched between her fingers like a white flag.

"I agree completely." Noah started the car and waved. "I'll see you around five."

Starr growled wordlessly as he drove away. She kicked the concrete curb, then hopped around with her foot smarting. Of all the impossible, *frustrating* men in the world, Noah Bradley was the worst.

"'*I know,*'" she mimicked to the deserted street. "He doesn't know *anything*. He thinks he's got me all figured out, but he doesn't. He doesn't have a clue."

Turning, Starr limped back to the gate and up the walk to the house. She opened the door of the shop and stepped inside, automatically taking a deep breath. She'd done that as a child, always wondering what kind of concoction her parents had mixed up and decided to call dinner. Over the years the scents had become a pleasant combination of herbs and fragrant oils, yeast and the faint aroma of the wool her mother spun and wove into artistic patterns.

"Starr?"

Across the room she saw her parents standing shoulder to shoulder, dismayed expressions creasing their faces. They shook their heads in unison.

"He wears suits," said her father.

"Darling," her mother murmured sadly, "a doctor?"

Incredible. Putting a hand to her stomach, Starr dropped into a chair and dissolved into laughter.

Noah was right, they *had* been spying.

Chapter Four

The doorbell rang as Noah finished checking the temperature on the hot tub. A vaguely satisfied expression crossed his face. *Right on time.*

He'd struggled with his conscience all day. Back and forth, a dozen contrary arguments. Deep down he wanted to see Starr again. Sexual attraction was a funny thing, stubbornly deaf to all the reasonable arguments in the world. And there was nothing reasonable about Starr. She was pure heart-stopping, risk-taking *trouble*. A prudent man didn't get involved with a woman like that. He just didn't.

But he still wanted to see her again.

Oh, well. Noah shrugged to himself. It wasn't like they were getting married or anything. Right? He opened the door with a flourish and smiled at Starr. Her eyes widened. "Do you like it?" Noah asked, fingering one of the many holes in his faded sweatshirt. The sweatshirt had seen better days. In fact, it had seen better decades.

Starr put her hand over her mouth and smothered a laugh. Noah's top was only slightly more respectable than his cutoffs. There were holes in his patches, barely distinguishable color remained in the worn denim and ragged strings hung from the ragged fringe. And he was barefoot. He could have passed for the worst beach bum she'd ever laid eyes on. Except most beach bums didn't have Noah's basic appeal. Broad shoulders, flat stomach, strong legs...killer smile.

"Is that the latest in yuppie fashions?" she asked when she could trust her voice.

"I thought you'd be impressed." He stepped back and made a broad gesture, inviting her inside.

Starr sauntered past, trying not to appear too curious. From the outside the house was subtly different from the others along the coast. A lot more private, for one thing. The house was hidden behind a stand of trees, which hadn't been clear-cut during construction. Some of the other places stuck out like sore thumbs, as though to say the owners were impressive and well-off. She had no doubt the *interiors* of those houses were equally pretentious.

As Noah led her to the back of the house, her eyes widened farther. Aside from Becky's toys scattered about, the decor was quite simple, with lots of plants and soft lighting. Very tranquil, even if it was—understandably—masculine.

He caught her wide-eyed gaze and grinned. "What did you expect? Bachelor pad etchings?"

"Not exactly." Starr gazed around the room. "I...uh, thought upwardly mobile professionals collected pre-Columbian art or African artifacts...or something."

Noah whistled and stuck his hands in his back pockets. Starr swallowed because she could see the smooth flex of his muscles through the gaping holes in his sweatshirt. *Get a grip,* she ordered silently. *You're salivating over a yuppie for pity's sake.*

"You're a cynic," he announced. "Must be an occupational hazard."

She wrinkled her nose. "More like a backlash from my childhood. My parents are loving, optimistic people. They're so certain of the world's ultimate goodness, I became a cynic out of pure self-defense."

"That explains things." The twinkle in his brown eyes made a warm, shivery sensation coil through her body.

"Where's Becky?" she asked, looking around again. Except for the sound of waves breaking on the rocks below the bluff, the house was unusually quiet. It seemed odd, because even one child could make a lot of noise.

"She's in her bedroom, playing with Kitty."

"I'd like to see her."

Noah looked at her for a long moment, his expression unreadable. "Okay. Come with me."

Starr followed and he paused at an open door. Gathering her courage, she slipped around him and saw Becky in the corner, playing with Kitty.

She knelt next to her goddaughter, trying not to look like a novice to Noah—even though she was a complete amateur when it came to children. She was okay in the short run, but long-term frightened her.

"Hi there. My name is Starr. I'm…uh…your godmother. Do you remember me?"

Becky nodded with an angelic smile. "Kitty."

"That's right. I got your kitty for you."

Becky pointed to the feline, who was gazing raptly at a hamster rolling across the floor in a small plastic exercise ball. The feral gleam in Kitty's eyes suggested he'd like to get his fangs on that small morsel. When the ball rolled in his direction he stopped it with his paw and hovered over it, breathing heavily.

"Er…Noah?" Starr said quickly.

He gave her a wry grin. "Don't worry, that ball is indestructible. Tippy doesn't even notice Kitty. Watch, you'll see."

Sure enough, the hamster settled down and began pulling sunflower seeds from the pouch in his cheeks. He was quite unconcerned about the jaws of doom salivating over his little world.

"O'ood Kitty," Becky announced. She gazed at the cat with approval, apparently thinking Kitty was just being friendly.

After a few minutes, Noah said something about checking dinner, and vanished, leaving them alone. Which was a relief; if she was going to be awkward with the child it was better without an audience. In Starr's limited experience she'd found kids much more tolerant than adults.

"Shall we play a game?" she asked, sitting down and settling her green silk skirt over her legs.

Becky didn't say anything, just pulled a game from her toy box. The game involved picking various shapes and dropping them through the correct slots. Starr handed her a circle and Becky pushed it through the circular hole, doing equally well with a five-pointed star. But when it came to the square piece she picked the triangular slot.

"Try another hole," Starr suggested finally.

Becky shook her head and tried to hammer the square into submission with a toy mallet. Her small face was focused with a single-minded determination...an expression reminiscent of Noah.

Starr sighed. What was wrong with her? She was supposed to be thinking about Becky, not Becky's uncle.

"Becky, can you play patty-cake?" The child looked up from her hammering, but her mouth remained stubbornly closed. "How about...?" Starr glanced around the room, searching for an alternative. There was an abundance of expensive toys, including interactive, computerized teaching games. Everything a little girl needed.

And from under the edge of the eyelet dust ruffle on the bed, peeked the toe of a large brown shoe. Leaning over, Starr flipped up the ruffle. A second shoe was hidden behind the first, and draped over both was a creased silk tie. She explored further and came up with a second tie.

She pulled them out, smiling idiotically at the image they brought to mind—Noah, tired from work, coming first to Becky's room to play with her for a while. Sweet. "Hmm. See what I found, Becky?"

The youngster nodded.

"Where do these go? Like this?" Starr put her fingers in the shoes and pretended to walk around on her arms.

"Sooz."

"Oh…that's right, they're shoes." She hid her pleasure at getting a response. "Are they yours? Here, let's see." She rose to her knees and lifted Becky into the shoes.

Becky giggled. "Unca Noah sooz."

"How about this?" Starr dropped one of the ties about her goddaughter's neck, and wrapped the other around her waist like a sash. By then Becky was giggling so hard, she plopped down on her bottom.

"What are you doing in my clothes?" Noah said, surprising them both.

"Thilly," said Becky, still chortling with pleasure. She patted Starr's cheek with her tiny fingers.

"Yes, she is silly," he agreed, his eyes bright with laughter.

Starr caught her breath. She'd seen the warmth in his smile before, but nothing like this…unreserved and hot enough to melt the polar ice caps. Becky was his brother's child, but she had Noah's smile.

"We're playing. You're supposed to be silly when you're playing," she said with pretend indignation.

"I see. Can we be silly, too?" Noah sat beside them and gently tickled Becky on the tummy. She tried to tickle him back, and before they knew it all three of them were rolling on the carpet, laughing.

"I'm not sure we're setting a good example," Starr gasped when she could think again—no easy task with Noah's legs tangled with hers and his hips hard against her bottom. Funny, she'd never noticed the pleasant contrast between a man and woman...softness against muscles and hair-roughened skin.

Pleasant? What an understatement. It was as erotic as hell. Noah could give lessons in seducing inhibited women.

"Oh?" His breath fanned across her neck and she got that shivery feeling again...an aching, tense shiver clear to the base of her stomach. "No roughhousing, huh?"

Starr pulled the toy mallet from under her shoulder, wincing a little. "What do you think?"

"I think you feel good," Noah whispered, trailing his fingers down her hip. "Silk...that's nice." But his hand lingered on her bare thigh where the thin fabric of her dress had ridden up. "Very nice."

"Stop it," she breathed.

"I wish I could," he muttered. "You're tough on good intentions, lady."

Her gaze darted to Becky, who was pulling on two of Noah's toes with considerable effort. She was so little, and Noah was so careful of her, so protective. Starr blinked. Anyone looking at them the past few minutes would have thought they were a family. Mom and dad and baby.

Dangerous thought. Domesticity didn't have any place in her life. Even with her ex-husband they'd never pretended to have a normal kind of marriage. Neither of them had wanted that. Well…Starr bit her lip and considered. Chase had talked about getting a house in the country, but that's all it was—talk. They were too restless to settle in one place.

Noah's finger traced her ear and she gulped. "What are you thinking?" he murmured.

"Actually, about my ex-husband," she said honestly.

He stiffened. *Really* stiffened. She could feel him tense from head to toe…including the toe Becky was pulling on. Now that was an interesting response. She didn't have the slightest idea what it meant, but it was interesting.

"Just how long *were* you married?" he drawled.

"A while." She untangled her legs and sat up, straightening her dress.

"How long is 'a while'?"

Starr darted a glance at him. "If you must know, six months. The divorce took a lot longer."

His jaw dropped. "Six months? That's not very long."

"Thanks for the analysis." She got to her feet and ruffled Becky's hair before walking to the door. "Like I didn't know."

For a second Noah closed his eyes, groaning at his wayward tongue. If he'd been more diplomatic he'd still have Starr nestled against him. God, he was dumb. Dumb for speaking up, dumb for regretting the playful intimacy he'd lost.

"Unca Noah?"

"Yes?" Becky was gazing at him, a small doubt in her face. Despite her age, she was quite sensitive to the moods of the adults around her. "It's all right, sweetheart. We're getting ready for dinner. Do you want to feed Kitty?"

She nodded and he caught her up in his arms.

"Okay."

They found Starr in the living room. She was staring out

at the ocean, her arms folded protectively across her body. Noah sighed quietly. Kissing her had been a big mistake. And rolling around on the floor together had been inflammatory. But she'd looked so sweet playing with Becky that he'd forgotten himself.

Then he'd touched her and all she could think about was her ex-husband. Did that mean she was still hung up on him? Just because a marriage hadn't worked out, it didn't mean they'd stopped loving each other.

"Starr?"

She half turned. "Yes?"

"I…uh…are you all right? I didn't mean to upset you." Noah shifted Becky against his hip and waited. For an instant Starr seemed bewildered, then she lifted her shoulders. "I'm fine. It's just embarrassing, having your marriage fall apart so quickly. It should have been perfect—even our careers fit together."

"What happened?" he asked, before he could think better of the question.

"Nothing." Her smile turned sad. "Absolutely nothing."

Becky tugged at his shirt…her way of saying she was bored with this adult conversation. "Down."

"Okay." Noah lowered her to her feet and she ambled away through the dining area. It was just as well; his tongue was becoming quite unruly around Starr—she had a terrible effect on him. "Nothing happened…was that also in bed?"

Starr's mouth opened and closed several times and her eyes turned emerald, matching the shimmering green silk of her dress. "That's none of your business," she finally sputtered.

Of course it wasn't his business, and he couldn't even blame his professional instincts. He wanted to know because he was a man…and because Starr made him feel more restless than he'd felt in a long time. "I just..." His voice trailed off and he shrugged.

She rolled her eyes and stalked past him. "I'm hungry. I thought you were going to feed me dinner."

Strikeout.

"I hope you're not expecting anything gourmet," he said, following her into the kitchen. "I'm pretty limited in my cooking."

She muttered something in an unknown language—it didn't sound polite. Wonderful. It was a perfect reminder they had nothing in common. Starr had lived in foreign countries most of her adult life; he had lived in medical school, taken his residency in the city, then moved to Astoria. Even before he'd gotten custody of Becky, he certainly hadn't been interested in living out of a suitcase.

Big difference. A *huge* difference. He handed Becky a small cup of milk to pour in Kitty's bowl. "By the way, did you bring your swimsuit?" he asked casually.

Her nose wrinkled. "Yes. But I can't believe you have a hot tub. It's so...trendy."

Trendy? That didn't sound good, at least not the way she'd said it. "They aren't as common in the Pacific Northwest as some places," he said. "And this one is special."

"How can a hot tub be special? A Jacuzzi is a Jacuzzi. You get in, you get out. What else is there?"

A lot of possibilities occurred to Noah—most of them centered around getting in and out of the water *together*. Sharing a hot tub, bathtub or even a washtub with Starr would be spectacular from any point of view. She had a body that would tempt a saint, and however annoying, the defiant sparkle in her blue-green eyes would ensure life never got boring.

"It's out on the deck, overlooking the ocean—very

peaceful. And I didn't get it because it was popular, I got it because I like hot tubs.''

"Uh-huh.''

Noah could tell she wasn't convinced. "Don't think so much," he advised. "After you get in you'll discover it isn't so bad. I'll even open a bottle of wine...which beats herbal tea, anyday.''

Wine? Starr gulped.

What a lovely image. A family dinner, followed by putting the baby to bed, and then the steamy intimacy of a hot tub, replete with wine. Her negative view of hot tubs took a sudden turnabout. They might be the ultimate badge of yuppiness, but they also had some appealing aspects she'd never considered.

She leaned down to scratch Kitty behind the ears as he lapped his milk. A voiceless growl rose from his furry chest.

"I don't want your food," she scolded.

"He doesn't care," Noah murmured. "Er...hang on for a while. I just remembered Tippy—he needs to go back in his home.''

Thankfully he was gone for a few minutes, which gave her a chance to catch her breath. Hot tubs? Wine? She was losing her mind; there wasn't any other explanation. Why else would that sound so appealing, along with everything else? Even Tippy was kind of sweet.

Starr frowned thoughtfully. A hamster?

"I wouldn't have guessed you were the hamster and aquarium type," she said when Noah returned. "Maybe a fancy saltwater aquarium, but not that tropical fish monstrosity in the living room.''

"I beg your pardon, it is *not* a monstrosity.''

"Well..." She made an apologetic gesture. "It's so big.

And there's all that cute stuff inside, like the scuba diver with bubbles coming out of his helmet.''

"You mean I'm not the 'cute' type?"

Starr shrugged, some improper thoughts racing about in her head. Cute? Sure, Noah was cute, though that wasn't the kind of "cute" they'd been talking about. He stood there, slouched against the door frame with his hands tucked in the pockets of his ragged cutoffs...looking utterly male and compelling. She'd never been so intoxicated by just looking at a man—it was strange and exciting and *stupid.*

"Actually," he said after a moment, "Becky wanted the aquarium and hamster. She likes animals.''

The corner of her mouth twitched. And whatever Becky wanted, Becky got. Like Kitty. She supposed it was natural for a parent to go overboard, spoiling a new child. Noah plainly adored his niece and he'd made drastic changes in his life to make a home for her. There weren't a lot of people who would do that.

He raised an eyebrow at her continued silence. "What?"

"You're a nice man, Noah Bradley," she said softly.

His mouth dropped and a dull red crept under his skin. "I...er...thanks."

Their gazes locked for a long minute and sharp awareness slid through Starr. She'd never done things in the usual way. Dating. Falling in love. Making a home. In her marriage, she and Chase had been like two electrons whizzing around the center of an atom, always moving but never together.

So what was she doing here? Asking for the impossible?

With a final searching glance Noah stepped away from the door. Starr swallowed hard. This was ridiculous. Absolutely ridiculous. She was getting out of control, she had to make it clear she wasn't available in any way—not that

Noah was interested in a permanent relationship. He might be attracted to her, but he also disapproved of everything she represented.

Luckily Becky didn't notice her preoccupation. She cheerfully fed Kitty his dry cat food piece by piece, while Noah stir-fried shrimp and asparagus, refusing Starr's help because she was "the guest." Being treated like "the guest" just frustrated her more because it underscored his intention to hold her at arm's length from Becky—or else he didn't trust her cooking.

"You've been awfully quiet."

Starr shifted her feet uncomfortably. They'd eaten a delicious meal, played with Becky, then gotten her to bed. She really ought to be leaving—her concern was Becky, not Becky's uncle.

Noah flipped a switch on the wall and the living room became a dark cave, illuminated solely by the glimmering light from the aquarium.

Self-consciously, Starr brushed her hair away from her face. "I should go home."

"It's early. Besides, you haven't tried the hot tub."

"Yes, but—"

"Use the bathroom down the hall," he said, cutting off her protest. "I'll take the cover off the tub while you're changing."

Her jaw dropped as he disappeared, without ever seeming to rush. Lord, the man moved quietly. He could sneak up on your heart without you ever realizing it.

Unbelievable.

Starr's fingernails dug into her palm. What was she thinking? It was as though she'd been turned into a raging romantic. She sank down on the couch and stared at the aquarium. Becky's aquarium. Teeming with brightly colored fish, a shipwreck, treasure chest and divers with bubbly helmets—it was the kind of display she would have laughed about a month ago, but now thought was rather darling. And the hot tub sounded wonderful.

She slumped deeper in the butter-soft leather cushions.

No way. She wasn't going out and getting in that Jacuzzi. Her brain was being infected with yuppiness. It was a disease. She didn't have to be a yuppie to be a part of Becky's life. In fact, Becky would be better off with exposure to other life-styles.

"Starr?" Noah murmured, pulling open the sliding glass door to the patio.

"Go away."

"This is my house." A thread of laughter was woven through the words.

"Then I'll go away."

"No, you won't," he said firmly. "You're tense and you need to relax."

"You're not my doctor."

"I know. But if you don't come with me, I'm going to carry you." He stepped farther into the house, silhouetted by moonlight.

Starr groaned. That's all she needed. Noah had discarded his sweatshirt and all that lay between him and his birthday suit was a ratty pair of cutoffs…and from what she could see in the silver light, it was a pretty magnificent birthday suit.

"I don't want to be a yuppie," she grumbled.

He crouched next to her, a mixture of warmth and the freshness of an evening breeze. "I'm not asking you to be anything. But you're edgy and tired from that hectic life of yours. What's wrong with a little relaxation? That's the point of a vacation, right?"

"Yes," Starr said slowly.

Noah slid his forefinger around her right ankle and pulled off her sandal. Taking her foot in both hands he massaged the arch.

"Don't," she mumbled, though the massage felt terrific. She'd love a massage like that everyday. It was typically Noah—strong and gentle at the same time.

"Where's your swimsuit?" he asked without missing a stroke.

"Under my clothes."

"Really? That's interesting. I guess all you have to do is untie this thing at your waist and then you're ready."

Before Starr could stop him, Noah had tugged open the closure of her wraparound dress. "Stop that."

Frantically she tried to keep the slippery fabric in place, but Noah was bigger and stronger and faster. And he had another advantage—he wanted to win, a lot more than she did.

As Starr shifted in the deep couch to get some leverage, one of her hands slipped between the cushions.

"Yuck," she yelped.

Noah paused. "What's wrong?"

She pulled out her fingers and sniffed the gooey mess covering them. "Peanut butter. And strawberry jam, I think."

Their eyes met—just before they started laughing.

"Shhh, quiet," she choked out between chuckles. "We'll wake Becky."

"Well, it's her peanut butter."

"Wretch." Starr scrambled inelegantly off the couch, trying to keep her sticky hand in the air. "Help," she finally ordered, only to have Noah plant his hand on her bottom and push. It helped…but it also turned her legs into jelly, and she toppled over him.

"I like that," he said cheerfully.

He would. In retaliation she slid her jam-smeared fingers down his bare back. It didn't stop him; he just wriggled until she was firmly astride his hips, trapped between his body and the softness of the leather cushions. Then he kissed her throat, which didn't make it right, but certainly felt nice.

"Noah, I have to get up."

"Are you going to Jacuzzi with me?"

"That sounds kinky. I'm not doing anything kinky." Starr put the palms of both her hands on his shoulders and shoved. It was like pushing at a sun-warmed stone wall.

He tipped his head back. "I just realized something—you're a prude."

She stopped pushing and glared. "I am not. That's a terrible thing to say."

"Okay, have it your way. I just want to relax in the hot tub. *With you.*"

"All right. Just back off!"

He finally released her, a smug smile on his face. "Let's go."

"I have to get cleaned up," she protested.

"Okay…the Jacuzzi's on the right side of the deck. You have ten minutes."

"Bossy, bossy," Starr muttered. She kicked off her other sandal and hurried to the bathroom to wash her fingers. Her dress was lost in the bowels of his couch, and was probably covered with jam, as well.

Yuck. She took a damp towel and wiped away the remaining stickiness, making faces at her reflection. Her swimsuit was made of a space-age fabric guaranteed not to drip, or at least that's what the manufacturer's label had claimed.

"Drat," Starr muttered, leaning closer to the mirror. She hadn't realized the low neckline didn't hide the wound on her shoulder, and in the bright vanity light the mark looked particularly ugly. Tugging didn't help; the strap was too narrow and wasn't cut the right way. The dim light in the living room must have kept Noah from noticing the scar, but she couldn't count on getting lucky all evening.

All at once she smiled. She'd borrow something from Noah—he owed it to her, after all.

Two minutes later she walked out on the deck, effectively covered by one of Noah's shirts. The tails reached below her knees, and the sleeves had to be rolled up, but it was a perfect disguise.

"Over here."

Starr followed his voice and the sound of churning water, shivering in the night breeze. "It's cold."

"Not in here."

The hot tub was set in the far corner of the deck, banked by plants on two sides. A bottle of wine and two glasses sat on the edge. Very intimate and sensual, like Noah. He obviously enjoyed his senses—fine wine, supple leather and silk...the velvet sweep of hot water and the crashing of ocean waves. But she wasn't like that, and she had to tell him before he got the wrong idea.

"Uh...Noah. There's something you should know."

Her teeth chattered and he sat forward. "You're going to freeze out there. And what is that *thing* on you?" He made it sound as if she was covered in a horse blanket.

"I borrowed one of your shirts."

"I see."

"What about Becky?" she asked. "She's alone in the house. I should stay in there."

"Starr!" Noah sounded exasperated and he pointed to an object on a nearby bench. "That's a baby monitor, turned on high volume. And there's an alarm rigged into the monitor if she opens her door. For that matter, the whole house is wired, and I've got every cupboard and drawer childproofed. You don't think I'd sit out here and take a chance of Becky getting hurt, do you?''

"No...of course not."

Unable to think of another excuse, Starr stepped into the steaming water, smoothing the shirt down as it billowed around her. Quite deliberately she sat opposite Noah and tried to wedge herself into stillness. It was impossible. The water swirled madly, brushing their legs together and constantly pushing her away from the side. She'd only been in a Jacuzzi one other time in her life, and she didn't remember it being such a problem. Although...she'd never been in one with Noah Bradley before, either.

"What did you want to tell me?" he murmured. He seemed to be floating a lot more comfortably than she was doing.

"Umm..." Her bare foot brushed his thigh and she pulled away sharply, splashing water on them both. "I might as well confess...I'm no good at this."

"What? Hot tubbing?" He smiled.

"I think you were right, I am a prude," Starr said quickly. "I don't sleep around and I'm not good at...uh...sex." There, she'd said it, and it was just as humiliating as she'd expected the confession to be. "I'm mean, I'm okay up to a certain point, but nothing happens."

For a startled minute Noah stared at her, then he laughed.

"This isn't funny." She kicked him. "It isn't what broke up my marriage, but it certainly didn't help."

"I'm not laughing at that." He chuckled again. "It's the way you said it...'I'm not good at sex.'"

"Okay, what did you want me to say—'By the way, I'm frigid, so don't get your hopes up'?" Starr threw out her hand, fighting frustrated tears. "I have my parents on one side, always talking about love and the glorious, grand passion of life. And there's all these other people out there, falling in love and making families and building houses with three-car garages. I don't have that kind of passion. It doesn't work for me."

Her wild flow of words were choked into silence as Noah loomed over her and put his fingers across her lips.

"I'm sorry," he murmured. "Starr...there's no such thing as being frigid, just two people who aren't right for each other. As for passion, I think you have more passion than any woman I've met. You just haven't focused it in that particular direction."

She sniffed. "I'm thirty-two, not a teenager frightened by her first encounter. If it hasn't happened by now, I doubt it's going to."

"Have you ever slowed down long enough to find out?"

Starr sighed. "Photography is a tough way to make a living—I can't afford to slow down."

"Tonight you can." He leaned over and turned a switch, transforming the rushing bubble of the water into a soft swirl. "Don't think so much. Just relax."

Irritation flashed through her. "Don't pull that superior 'I know what's best' routine. I only said that stuff so you wouldn't get the wrong idea. It's my fault because I kissed you first, so now I'm being honest and telling you the truth."

He didn't say anything for a while; then she heard a quiet sigh. "I'm not trying to be superior. We just have a difference of opinion. You're a talented, intelligent woman, who I happen to think would be dynamite in bed."

She slumped in the water, feeling foolish. "Thank you."

"My pleasure." Noah slid his hand behind her back and rubbed her tight muscles. "Don't worry," he whispered. "I'm just being a good host."

"Humph," Starr mumbled, trying not to show how much

she liked Noah Bradley touching her. Jeez, she *really* liked it. The kind of ''like'' that made women do nutty things. She knew what it led to—commitment, marriage, children and being tied down in one place for the rest of her life. Strangely though, the constricting panic she'd always felt at the prospect didn't seem as bad. Maybe she was getting soft.

And maybe she'd lost her mind. Marriage and sex were the only things she'd ever completely failed at doing. She'd already blown one marriage with a man who understood her work. What chance did she have with a man like Noah, who disliked reporters of any kind? The answer was zero.

''If you have to hold on to something, hold on to me,'' he said, tugging her fingers away from the edge of the hot tub. ''Trust me, I won't let you drown.''

''That's silly.'' But she let him support her, one arm beneath her neck, her bottom resting across his knees. Through the steam rising from the water she could see stars glittering in the night sky.

Noah reached out and plucked something from a hanging plant, then brushed it across her lips. It was cool and velvety, like the petals of a rose.

''What's that?''

''A fuchsia blossom.'' He traced her face and neck with the flower, taking his time, letting her enjoy the whispering caress.

''It doesn't have a fragrance.''

''No.'' Noah lifted his knees and Starr rolled closer, boneless from the relaxing warmth of the water. It was like before, when he'd kissed her. Hot and steamy. *Safe.*

She wasn't even aware he'd unfastened the buttons of her borrowed shirt until the edges flowed away. But she knew her breasts tingled with a funny kind of ache. For the first time she wanted a man to really touch her, to do...a lot of things.

"Noah?"

He kissed her. A kiss as soft as the blossom he'd teased her with. It wasn't *nearly* enough and the fink probably knew it, too. Noah had a terribly unfair advantage—not only had he studied human biology in medical school, he was instinctive about this kind of thing. Instincts were great things. They kept you alive and breathing. If she had better instincts she wouldn't have to think everything out ahead of time.

Noah's fingers brushed across her breasts and her brain short-circuited. He might be right about her thinking too much.

"Do you like that?"

"Like it? What do you think?" she said thickly, all too aware of the sensual weight of her breasts, and the hard swell of her nipples beneath the thin fabric. Her swimsuit was a joke. She might as well be naked.

And she wanted... Starr's eyes widened as Noah drew the flower across her breasts and up one shoulder. She was caught in a sensual vise, unable to move, unable to breathe, unable to imagine being anywhere else. They were in the center of a mist-filled universe.

All at once the silken glide of petals hesitated as Noah stiffened, making her aware of hard muscles and the roughness of wet denim beneath her thighs.

"Noah?"

"Your shoulder." He sounded distant, angry.

Starr blinked. Her shoulder? What about her shoulder?

His fingers—no longer seductive, but skilled like a doctor—probed the tender scar next to her heart.

Damn.

Chapter Five

"I told you I'd been shot," Starr said calmly.

"Shot? You said *a while back*. You knew I'd think it was at least a couple of years ago."

"Well, it wasn't."

Noah abruptly dumped her into the deep center of the water and she came to the surface spluttering. "Great. I've survived wars, wild animals and tornadoes, and now I get drowned in a Jacuzzi."

"Lady, you're dangerous." He swung out of the tub and dried himself with a towel.

"That isn't fair." Starr slid along the tiled bottom and caught his arm. "I didn't want to talk about it. It happened and it's over."

He tossed the towel away. "Are there any other little surprises I should know about? Was that the first time you were shot? And when was the last time you were attacked by wolves, or fell through the floor of a burning building?"

Starr released Noah's arm and lifted her chin. "For your

information, there's never been a documented case of a healthy wolf attacking a human being.''

''And you should know, right?''

''I can't believe I'm discussing this with you. It's not that big a deal.''

''My God, Starr, you were almost killed. Not a 'big deal.''' Noah snorted. ''Another fraction of an inch and you'd be dead.''

''But I'm fine. And you're exaggerating, anyway. It wasn't that close.''

''That isn't the point.'' He leaned over her, angry and overwhelming in the steamy darkness. ''You're planning on going back, right?''

''Uh…yes. Of course. It's my work, remember?'' Starr's heart skipped painfully, because for a fraction of a second she'd almost said *no*.

No to the excitement of foreign lands and their inhabitants.

No to a dreary succession of hotels and dusty local airlines.

She sank lower in the water, shivering from the cold night air. And from uncertainty. Blast Noah Bradley, anyway. He didn't have any right to question her life. She'd always been certain about her future, about what she wanted.

''Becky's lost enough,'' he snapped. ''She needs stability.''

Something brushed Starr's hand and she opened her fingers. In the faint light she could see the fuchsia blossom Noah had caressed her with, now wilted by the warm water. Crushed. Tears brimmed in her eyes and she held it carefully in her palm.

''Don't use Becky as an excuse,'' she said bitterly. ''You got too close and now you're backing off.''

"You don't know what you're talking about."

"Really?" Starr wanted to scream or hit something. "It was just us in this water. Two adults. You might be worried about Becky, but that's only part of it. A small part, I might add."

He glared.

"You're so damned superior about everything. I know how much you miss your brother. You don't want to risk losing anyone else, but do you think you have the corner on emotions? On grief?"

"You didn't even come to the funeral."

Her knee slammed against the underwater bench as she stood up, but Starr only distantly registered the pain. "You want to know what happened?" She threw the crushed flower in his face and he jerked reflexively. "I was working in Africa, out of touch with everyone. When I got back I was rushed to my next assignment. It took months for my mail to catch up with me, but by then I was in the hospital. They didn't know who I was at first, and after that I kept my identity secret because I like my privacy."

"You should have called." Noah raked his hand through his hair.

"There aren't a lot of telephones out in a game preserve," she said sarcastically. "Or bathrooms, or kitchens, or hot tubs, or anything else."

"Wow, that makes me feel a lot better. So when Becky wants to know what happened to her godmother I can expect a delay of several months before learning if you're dead or alive."

"That does it!" Starr yelped, a barely repressed scream. She struggled out of his shirt and threw the sopping mess in his direction. Prepared this time, he easily evaded the missile and it thudded on the side of the house. "I don't need you to criticize my life. I told you I'd stay in contact with Becky. That's all you need to be concerned about.''

''Be reasonable,'' he snarled.

''I knew you wouldn't understand—that's why I didn't try to explain before.''

She scrambled out of the hot tub, uncertain of her footing and too furious to care. Noah tried to grab her and she instinctively kneed him—not *too* hard, but enough to make him let go. Hell, at least *those* instincts were working.

''Damnation,'' he groaned, just as she slipped on the deck and sat hard on her bottom.

''Serves you right.'' Starr kicked at him and tried to roll over.

''Oh, no, you don't, wildcat.'' The next thing she knew he was lying across her, holding her arms and preventing her from doing anything but spitting in his face. And she was angry enough to do just that.

''Let me go!''

''Not a chance. I value my various body parts a lot more than you do.''

Starr opened her mouth, then shut it quickly. *One* of Noah's body parts was pressed against her thigh, and it didn't seem to be inhibited by the blow she'd landed. ''Get off of me.''

''Not until I get my breath.''

She didn't want to wait, especially with the treacherous heat building in her abdomen.

Damn Noah. Damn his ragged cutoffs. And damn his sexy smile. That was the worst part—she still wanted him to touch her. She still wanted *him*.

And she'd thought sizzle wasn't that important.

Huh. Her reasoning had been *way* off the mark.

Making love with Noah Bradley wouldn't be just a few seconds of elusive pleasure…and she wouldn't care about messing up the bed. It would be mind-boggling, fabulous, Fourth of July fireworks and everything.

Starr shuddered. It would have been safer not to know how much Noah could make her feel, better not to experience any of these emotions. They were too powerful, too overwhelming.

"Leave me alone," she whispered.

The moon was higher now, casting a luminous light across the deck. Noah looked down at Starr and his heart wrenched. She looked so bewildered and hurt. He could only blame himself. His reaction had been way out of proportion. Yet even as he remembered, the same twisting fear tightened his chest—she'd almost died.

Starr was right. He wasn't just worried about protecting Becky, he was worried about protecting himself. It was too risky, caring about somebody who gambled with their life. Yet she stirred something deep inside his soul—the elemental need to mate and hold a woman as his own.

"Are you okay?" he murmured, brushing the damp strands of hair from her forehead.

"Noah, please don't...."

He put his lips over the inflamed scar on her shoulder and kissed it. Between the hot water and their fight, it must be throbbing. He'd seen her wince in pain several times in the past couple of days. No wonder—the wound wasn't fully healed, and thanks to Kitty's rescue, her skin was scattered with small scratches and claw marks.

How bad were they?

Noah eased the straps of Starr's swimsuit over her arms and felt her breathing quicken. Her eyes were closed, though he couldn't have read much in them in the moonlight. For just a moment he hesitated, then slowly drew the fabric down to her waist.

His own breathing accelerated.

Dear heaven. She was beautiful—her breasts firm and high, the crowns dark and drawn tight by the chill air. Her head was thrown back, eyes closed, the delicate lines of her face caressed by night shadows. A fairy, trapped by silver enchantment between the sky and ocean.

The tiny marks on her skin just seemed to emphasize her allure, by contrast drawing attention to the smooth satin mounds and velvet tips of her breasts.

Noah buried his face in the curve of Starr's neck. He'd never known anyone quite like her before. Frustrating and difficult. Defiant and unconventional. Restless. *Provocative.*

He couldn't help himself; he slid down and captured her nipples between his lips and fingers, drawing hungry little sounds from her throat.

Starr arched upward. Graceful. Sultry. The scent of her arousal seared across his mind. How could she have imagined she was unresponsive? Frigid? Utterly ludicrous.

"Starr," he groaned. He was burning, flayed alive with need.

She shifted, murmuring half-jointed words, and for an instant Noah thought she was rejecting him.

"My arms," Starr said, squirming, and he realized she was trapped by the swimsuit. He held the straps while she wiggled free, and a glorious minute later she clasped his shoulders, her fingers digging into the muscles of his back.

"Yes," he muttered, drawing her breast into his mouth, trying to hold as much of her as he could. He suckled deeply, tasting and claiming the sweet bud while she twisted beneath him.

He was only vaguely aware of her nails scoring his skin, then combing through his hair and tugging him upward. Reluctantly he released her, only to find a bounty of warmth and passion in her welcoming kiss.

"Starr…" He inhaled deeply, infusing himself with her

breath and essence, wanting more than he'd ever wanted from another woman.

The wood beneath his legs trembled faintly—as though from approaching footsteps—but he didn't care. He couldn't let go of Starr, or else she'd disappear. Only it wouldn't be fairy wings carrying her away, but an airplane.

"Now *this* would make a great photograph."

Noah froze, hoping he'd imagined that sardonic voice. He lifted his face a couple of inches above Starr and they stared into each other's eyes.

"But I don't think it could be run in the family newspaper. A supermarket tabloid, maybe."

Okay, it wasn't his imagination, which meant he only had one option—killing Rafe McKittrick. Preferably with his bare hands.

"I think we have company," Starr said quite unnecessarily.

"Dammit, McKittrick! What are you doing here?" Noah snarled, turning his head far enough to see a pair of shoes, just a few feet away.

"Well, for one thing, I'm not enjoying myself as much as you are."

Noah stiffened and felt Starr's fingernails digging into his shoulder blades. The faint pricks of pain punctuated the deeper, hard hunger in his body. "Sorry," he murmured regretfully.

"Don't get up," she whispered.

"What...oh!" Abruptly he realized her dilemma. With him lying over her, she was relatively unexposed. But if he moved... Noah groaned again, acutely aware of her bare breasts, soft and yielding against his chest. Maybe he'd be grateful for the interruption when he could think more clearly, but right now he could chew nails.

He turned his back to Rafe, shielding Starr, and helped

pull the damp suit over her arms. Though it was unintentional, his fingers grazed her nipples several times and she moaned beneath her breath.

Well...*maybe* unintentional. Starr was murder on his self-control.

When she was covered, Noah let his gaze sweep down her body, only to discover a dilemma of his own. The formfitting, silvery white fabric left nothing to the imagination—every nuance of her body was carefully detailed...from her tight, textured nipples to the intimate shadows at the apex of her thighs.

A single expletive whistled out of his mouth.

Starr lifted one eyebrow.

"You could be arrested wearing that thing," he said hoarsely.

"It's just a swimsuit."

"Only by the wildest stretch of the imagination."

"I'm still here," Rafe said conversationally. "In case you've forgotten. And it's cold."

"It's a lot colder down here," Noah hissed without looking around—which wasn't strictly true. He and Starr were wet and lying on a breezy deck in the middle of the night, but they hadn't been cold. Together they'd generated more steam than a hydroelectric plant.

"Hi, Rafe."

"Hey, kid."

Starr sat up and pushed her wet hair over her shoulders. "I'm glad to see you. We've been playing phone tag for over a week."

Stepping forward, Rafe helped her up. And into his arms. He kissed her full on the mouth with one hand on her slim waist and the other cupping her tight, scantily clad bottom.

Noah got up and scowled. "Why do you keep breaking into my house?"

The other man lifted his head. "Touchy, touchy. After a test of the security system, I can absolutely vouch it works better when you turn it on."

"I don't do that until I go to bed."

"Looked like you were pretty close to bed to me."

Unconsciously, Noah took a step toward him.

"I'm cold," Starr said hastily. She patted Rafe on the arm. "Let's go inside."

"Sure, kid."

Kid. That annoyed Noah. Starr was not a kid. She was a beautiful, successful woman. If *he'd* called her "kid," she probably would have flattened him with a right hook.

And it annoyed him even more when Rafe shrugged out of his jacket and draped it across her shoulders. Sure, he felt better having her safely covered, but it was *Rafe's* jacket surrounding her.

Nuts. He was nuts. Jealous over a woman he'd only known for a couple of days. As if he didn't have enough to deal with—caring for Becky, and making sure the McKittricks couldn't take custody away from him.

"I'm so sorry about Amelia," Starr murmured to Rafe as they walked into the living room. "You don't know how much."

"Yeah, I do." Rafe gathered her close for another hug, much more platonic this time. It was obvious he thought a great deal of Starr.

Noah closed the sliding doors and rested his fist on the glass for a brief instant. In Starr's voice had been all the pain and sorrow he hadn't been willing to hear before.

"How are your parents doing?" she asked. "I haven't been able to reach them."

Rafe shrugged. "You know the folks. They close themselves off from everyone. They want custody of Becky, but

Amelia and Sam's will was pretty specific about the arrangements they wanted.''

Noah turned around. ''Keep your voice down. You don't want to wake her up.''

Rafe snorted. ''If that kid's anything like her mother, she could sleep through an earthquake.'' He looked between Starr and Noah assessingly, and a cynical smile twisted his mouth. ''You could use a cold shower, Bradley.''

''Leave it alone,'' Noah snapped. It wasn't any secret—least of all to Starr—that he'd wanted to make love to her. And he certainly wasn't going to be embarrassed over the physical evidence. On the other hand, their relationship was private...or should have been if Rafe wasn't such a cold, manipulative Peeping Tom.

Rafe shrugged, looking unperturbed. ''Hell, pal, I know what I said this morning, only I didn't think you'd be such a fast worker.''

Starr frowned. *Fast worker?*

''This has nothing to do with this morning,'' Noah said, utterly disgusted. ''Now tell me what you want, and get out of here.''

''Umm...excuse me,'' Starr interrupted. ''What do mean by 'fast worker'? And what happened this morning?''

''Oh, I just suggested the good doctor might strengthen his position by getting married. I didn't know he'd hit on you. I mean, that photo in the paper was just a fluke, right?'' Rafe sat down with another smile.

She stared at Noah. ''Is that what tonight was all about?''

''No! Don't worry, I'm not interested in marrying you,'' he assured her quickly.

''I see.'' Starr didn't know what was worse, thinking Noah had some scheme in trying to seduce her, or knowing he was willing to seduce her, but didn't have any interest beyond a quick night of sex. "I'm sorry you think I'd make such a terrible wife."

"That's not what I said," he protested.

"I'll bet."

"You're not being rational. It has nothing to do with you. I just don't want to marry anyone. Besides, you don't want to settle down in Astoria any more than I want to get married. What about your career?"

Starr didn't care if she was being irrational, she just wanted to escape. It was one thing to admit to yourself that you weren't ideal wife material, quite another to learn the man you've almost made love with feels the same way. As for settling down, if she decided to "settle down," she'd damn well do it!

"Men," she spat venomously. She threw Rafe's coat on the floor. "Where's my dress?"

"The bathroom?" Rafe suggested with a bored yawn.

"Go to hell." Starr stumbled to the couch and shoved her hand between the cushions.

"Please, let's talk about this," Noah said urgently. He touched her shoulder and she slapped him away.

"Ditto to you, Dr. Bradley."

Her fingers encountered the silk dress and she yanked it free. The emerald green fabric was sadly wrinkled, but she pulled it on nevertheless. At least it had missed being smeared with peanut butter and strawberry jam.

She put her chin up. "I wish I could say it has been a pleasure," she said and stomped out.

As a grand exit, it fell flat, but she didn't care. What mattered was getting away from Noah Bradley before she did something stupid.

Like crying.

Noah glared at Rafe, reclining comfortably in his own favorite easy chair. "You'd better have a good reason for being here."

"I was delayed coming back. I thought I'd spend the night so I could see Becky."

"Think again."

"Calm down, Bradley. Starr won't stay mad, she never does—short fuse but no staying power. She'll reason things out and realize I'm to blame, not you."

"That isn't the point. Whose side are you on?"

Rafe sat forward, his eyes bleak. "I'm on Becky's side. The kid needs a mother."

"She has me."

"Not good enough."

Noah clenched his fists. By God, he hated the Mc-Kittricks. Every one of them. "The custody arrangement doesn't require me to get married. I thought you respected your sister's last wishes."

"Oh, I do. But that doesn't mean I won't look out for what's best for Becky. She needs a mother, and frankly, you need a wife."

Noah said a word he rarely used and Rafe clucked at him. Damnation, he had to get Starr to teach him some of her foreign curses; at least they wouldn't be identifiable. Of course, he might never see her again, considering the way she'd blasted out of his house. "What did you hope to achieve by alienating Starr?"

"I didn't alienate her." Rafe definitely looked smug. "I just made sure the idea of getting married was planted in her mind. She's a little stubborn."

Noah started to agree, then clamped his mouth shut. He didn't want to agree with anything. Granted, there were worse things than getting married to a woman like Starr, but he didn't want to get married.

Did he?

All at once his eyes narrowed and he looked at his uninvited guest suspiciously. Starr wasn't the only one to whom Rafe had given "ideas."

Chapter Six

Brilliant.

You were just brilliant.

Starr put her head back against her pillow and gazed at her dress from the previous evening. It looked kind of pathetic slung across the lamp shade.

Noah now knew—beyond the shadow of a doubt—that she had a terrible temper. Somehow it had a shorter fuse around him...though frustrated hormones might have had something to do with her explosion.

"Excuses, excuses," she muttered to herself.

She'd have to call and apologize. Starr was just working up to that unpleasant task when she heard a light tap on the door.

"Yes?"

"A delivery came for you, Morning Star," said her mother, wandering into the room.

"I didn't hear anyone."

"No, they came an hour ago. Poor thing..." Moon

Bright patted the succulent stems of an aloe vera plant on the dresser. "I meant to water you."

Starr snuggled deeper under the blankets. "Mom, what was delivered?" she asked patiently.

"Oh, my, I left it on the landing."

Moon Bright wandered out, then wandered back, hidden behind an enormous floral arrangement. Starr looked at it suspiciously. "Isn't it pretty?" her mother murmured.

Yes, it was pretty, and unusual, with long-stemmed bear grass accenting the flowers. Unstructured. "Put it on the table." Starr slid out of bed and pulled the card from the envelope.

"Do you know a good foot doctor? Mine seems to be stuck in my mouth. Can we start over? Noah."

Starr blinked, astonished.

Oh, dear. Men never liked to apologize, and Noah was making the gesture when it wasn't even his fault...well, not entirely. There was something alarming about a man that nice.

And to convince a florist to make a delivery first thing Sunday morning? That took some determination, though his concern might be over what she'd tell the McKittricks.

No. Starr shook her head. She wasn't going to think like a cynic. The realities and reasons could be worked out later. She'd never been sent flowers before, she wanted to enjoy the moment—even if it was a little old-fashioned and conventional. Conventional had some advantages.

"Morning Star?"

Starr hid a smile. Her mother had a funny expression on her face. This was hard on her. Moon Bright and Blue River weren't nearly as vague as they appeared; they just lived in their own world, following the creed of "Live And Let Live." But Live And Let Live was a tough philosophy when it applied to your own offspring. Sometimes impossible.

"They're from Noah Bradley," she explained, waving at the arrangement.

Faint consternation crossed Moon Bright's face. "Oh…the doctor."

The way she said "the doctor" sounded more like "the convict."

Starr smiled wryly. "It's all right, Mom, Noah isn't interested in getting married."

At least not to me, she added silently, still feeling an illogical sense of hurt. In the long run it was best that Noah had been honest, and it wasn't like she wanted to get married again. Right? Even Rafe…

Her eyes narrowed. *Rafe.* The rat was probably still laughing his head off. He never did anything without an ulterior motive. It must have tickled his twisted sense of humor to say those things, knowing what conclusions she'd draw.

"Are you all right, dear?" asked Moon Bright. "You have such an odd expression. Is your shoulder hurting? Should I make a mustard-and-flax-seed poultice for it?"

Starr forced herself to smile. An herbal poultice—her vegetarian mother's version of chicken soup. "Thanks, Mom, but I'm fine."

Moon Bright hesitated a moment before nodding and drifting out the door. Starr collapsed on the bed and stared at her bare legs. A bruise was developing over her knee where she'd slammed it in the hot tub, and she had a scar on her calf from a playful lion cub, but otherwise they weren't too awful. She'd even been whistled at a few times.

Did Noah like her legs? He'd said she looked great in her jeans. The tight ones.

"Argghh!" Starr pulled the blankets over her head, realizing she was acting like any normal woman attracted to a man. Correction, she was acting like any normal *teenager*.

Does he like me?

Does he think I'm pretty?

Will he call me tomorrow?

Jeez. That was really pathetic. She was regressing into puberty...the puberty she'd never experienced. As a teenager she'd scared off boys. Adolescent males weren't too keen on girls more interested in taking pictures than making out. And frankly, all that time ago she wouldn't have recognized a pass unless it was a football and hit her in the face.

Starr pushed back the bedding. She didn't have to act like a teenager—or anything else—around Noah. Sure, Noah Bradley made her feel soft and womanly...and *sexy*. But that didn't mean she was going to change her life.

Though irritating, Rafe's interference had helped define the situation. Noah didn't want a globe-trotting photographer as a wife...she could hardly blame him. And *she*—as the globe-trotting photographer in question—didn't want to get married. Besides which, the whole thing was ridiculous. They hardly knew each other.

"Thanks, Rafe," Starr muttered. Rational thinking aside, she still wanted to strangle him. Or Noah.

She plucked Noah's card from the table and read it again. He'd taken the first step, she'd have to take the second.

For Becky's sake. Right?

"Right," she mumbled. Noah's broad shoulders and killer smile had nothing to do with it.

Absolutely nothing.

Her foot touched something soft on the floor and she picked up her swimsuit. It was dry, but there was a faint scent of chlorine clinging to the thin fabric. *Hmm*. She'd take a shower and wash it out before calling Noah.

You never could know when you might need a swimsuit.

* * *

Noah poured milk into Becky's cup. The little girl took it and looked at him soulfully. "Kitty?"

"We'll give Kitty something later."

Becky's lip pouted, but she didn't say anything. He sighed. They'd had a difficult morning. He'd finally gotten her dressed, wearing mismatched shoes and socks, and delivered to Sunday school. That part hadn't been too bad.

Well, at least not worse than usual.

But afterward she hadn't wanted to go home...not without the giant tortoise the teacher had brought to show the class.

Noah sighed. Fred—as the teacher called him—was a gentle creature, who looked out at the world with blinking eyes and an amazing patience for being handled by excited children. Becky cried when Noah said "no" to Fred, but this time he'd been determined—the tortoise belonged to someone else. The answer was *no*.

As it turned out, Fred was for sale—the teacher's *other* job was managing a pet store.

The newest addition to the household was now ensconced in a palatial terrarium. Kitty had promptly climbed in to say hello, but Fred was no dummy. Head and legs had vanished, leaving Kitty pawing a twelve-inch armored shell.

Noah smiled at the memory. It was almost worth the money to see Kitty so frustrated.

The phone rang and he picked it up. "Wild Kingdom" was probably calling, hoping to film a safari in his house. "Hello?"

"Hi...it's me."

The velvet timbre of Starr's voice sent heat sliding through Noah's veins. He turned away from Becky and tucked the remote receiver under his chin. "Good morning."

"I called earlier, but no one was home."

"We went to the early service at church, then we had to make housing arrangements for Becky's new tortoise."

There was a long silence, and then Starr said, "Tortoise?" in a faint tone. "She already has the aquarium and a hamster."

"And a cat," Noah added, figuring it wouldn't do any good to dissemble. "Really though, Fred shouldn't be a problem. He's pretty big, but he lives in an enclosed space and has a built-in defense against Kitty."

"Uh-huh." She didn't sound entirely convinced.

"Actually, I kind of like Fred."

"You like…a tortoise?" There was another long silence. "Er, Noah," Starr said hesitantly, "I know it's difficult after everything Becky's been through, but shouldn't you put your foot down? She can't have everything."

"You're right, but things are getting better," Noah assured her, figuring it wasn't a total lie. "Today was a fluke. She wanted Fred, and the Sunday school teacher said 'Sure,' he was for sale." He shrugged, though Starr couldn't see him.

"I guess that didn't help."

"No. By the way, am I forgiven?" he asked, hoping to change the subject before she realized he'd become a *total* marshmallow around his niece.

"Actually, I wanted to apologize, too. I overreacted."

Noah stirred a pot of spaghetti on the stove. After a McDonald's Happy Meal, spaghetti was his best bet with Becky. She really loved the stuff, though she was never very hungry after drinking juice and eating graham crackers in the nursery.

"I didn't mean to insult you," he murmured into the

phone. "You're a beautiful lady. And we obviously...well, get along in the physical end of things."

"That's the *only* way we get along. It doesn't matter anyway. You were right—neither of us wants the commitment." Starr laughed lightly. "But thanks for the flowers. They're beautiful."

Noah frowned. He should be relieved Starr wasn't still angry. Relieved she hadn't gotten the wrong idea about them. Only, he wasn't relieved. He was purely annoyed she could brush off their passionate response to one another as though it was meaningless.

"Kitty," Becky said. She'd scooted down from her chair and stood looking at him, holding her plastic cup carefully between her hands.

"Just a minute, Starr." He shifted the receiver. "Becky, Kitty had his own breakfast, and he has a whole bowl of dry food. We'll give him a treat later. The vet said he shouldn't have too much milk anyway."

"Problem?" Starr queried.

"Just the usual," Noah said as he went to the refrigerator and pulled out a package of salad greens. Six months ago he would have been appalled at the thought of buying pre-cut lettuce. Now he'd learned it was a matter of survival.

"Becky wants to turn Kitty into the fattest cat in Oregon," he continued. "I—wait!" He dropped the portable phone and caught Becky's cup just as she upended it in the vicinity of Kitty's bowl. As a result they were both liberally splattered with milk.

Becky giggled, then giggled some more when Kitty began licking the white droplets from her fingers.

Noah surrendered. He rescued the receiver from the floor, sat down and put his feet up. "Becky now needs a bath," he said, explaining his outburst. "After that, we're going to McDonald's for lunch. Will you join us?"

"I...I'd love to."

"Good. We'll pick you up in an hour." He glanced at Becky, who was still being licked by Kitty. "Or maybe two."

An hour and a half later Noah pulled up in front of the store belonging to Starr's parents. Becky's child seat was in the rear seat, and she stared wide-eyed at the house with its overhanging eaves, the sun shining across the bountiful garden.

"I'll be right back. Stay here," he said unnecessarily. Becky still hadn't figured out a way to undo the child restraints herself, though it wasn't for lack of trying. She was a clever little monkey.

Her face puckered.

Uh-oh.

"It's all right," he assured quickly. "I'll be right outside the car. You'll see me every minute."

"Go," she demanded.

Noah grimaced. Becky was like that nursery rhyme...when she was good, she was very, very good; and when she was bad, she was horrid. He didn't want Starr to see him trying to stop a tantrum—it was bad enough she knew about all the animals. And it wasn't such a big deal—he was getting better handling Becky. No one became a perfect parent overnight.

"Go," she said again.

He capitulated. "Okay, we'll go together." He leaned over and unfastened the buckles holding her. Satisfied, she clambered over the seat and clung to his neck as he opened the door.

The house was as quiet and peaceful as it had been the first time he'd come to see Starr; the only difference was a small Closed sign in the window. Even mama cat still lounged on the porch; she held a squirming kitten between her paws, giving it a vigorous bath.

"Kitty," Becky crowed.

Noah turned to one side, blocking her view. That's all he needed—another kitty in his household.

Moon Bright answered his knock, her expression grave and a little disappointed. "Hello, Dr. Bradley," she said formally. But her face softened when she looked at the child in his arms. "Welcome, little one."

Becky stuck her thumb in her mouth and hid her face against Noah's chest. Great, he thought, dynamo one minute, shrinking violet the next.

"Sorry," he apologized. "Becky is shy around people she doesn't know."

Moon Bright touched the delicate crystal hanging from her neck. She watched the child in his arms with a palpable air of sadness. "So like her mother," she murmured, reminding him Starr's parents had been close friends with the McKittricks. Then Moon Bright smiled gently. "Do you want to see our rabbits, Becky? They'll like you very much."

Instantly Becky's head popped out. She didn't say anything, but her rapt expression indicated the rabbits would be a popular choice. Noah resigned himself to a longer visit than he'd expected.

They found Starr in the kitchen, sitting at a large table and surrounded by stacks of papers. She was chewing on the end of a pencil, staring intently at a calculator.

"Dr. Bradley is here," Moon Bright said, putting a hand on her daughter's shoulder.

Starr jumped. "Noah...I'm sorry, I meant to be ready when you got here." She smiled at Becky.

"No problem. I should have called before we left the house."

Starr rose to her feet, then lunged to catch a drifting pile of paper. She grabbed a clump of quartz crystals to weight the errant stack.

Moon Bright looked at the mess on her table and sighed. "So much fuss. Can't you take care of this another time, Morning Star?"

"No, I can't. You're in enough of a mess already."

"Blue River," the elder woman called. "Would you bring Aurora and her babies inside?"

"Mom! He's looking for last year's expense records."

"I know, dear. But Becky would like to play with the rabbits before you leave. Isn't that right, little one?"

The child gave a quick, bashful nod and Noah lowered her to the floor, at the same time exchanging a commiserating glance with Starr. He thought her parents were charming—he also thought they were pretty wacky.

"You were going to get an accountant this year," Starr said when her father arrived, his arms filled with twitching-nosed bunny rabbits instead of ledgers. "That's what we agreed to, remember?"

"We really meant to, darling. Time just got away. But you'll straighten everything out...you always do." He gave Starr a serene smile.

"Thanks, Dad," she said dryly. "But I still need those expense records to complete your tax return."

The rabbits hopped in opposite directions as soon as they were put on the ground. The elder couple and Becky chased them in ecstatic pursuit, oblivious to everything else. Starr just shook her head.

"It's the middle of June," Noah said in a low voice, pointing out the obvious—that her parents were well past the deadline to file their taxes.

For more than a minute Starr said nothing, but a series of emotions including frustration and wry acceptance chased across her face. "I know. They're two months late, they didn't apply for an extension, and they missed their estimated tax payments. I can only hope they lost money last year."

"Which is why you need the expense records."

She shrugged. "That, or a good lawyer. I attended my first audit when I was twelve. The auditor and I worked everything out, then he asked if I'd been adopted. I think the only reason he didn't put them in jail was because they were going home in my custody."

"I see." Noah strangled a laugh, because no matter how humorous she made things sound, it wasn't that funny. He also suspected Starr would be paying any taxes or fines if they had actually *made* money on their health food store…which didn't appear likely, considering their location and general lack of business acumen.

Sighing, Starr rubbed her temples.

"Headache?" Noah asked quietly. He put his hands on her shoulders. She jerked slightly, but didn't pull away.

"I'm fine."

One of his eyebrows lifted. Fine? She was tighter than wires on a suspension bridge. With firm, circular movements he began massaging her tense muscles. "You can use the hot tub later. It'll help you relax," he murmured in her ear.

Relax?

Starr swallowed convulsively. How did he expect her to relax with his warm breath fanning the side of her face? Or with his hands on her, awakening memories of fuchsia blossoms gliding across her skin like velvet, followed by sultry kisses? Still…at least he wasn't intentionally sending subtle, sexy reminders about the hot tub. *This* time he was being genuinely nice.

"Bunnies, go," Becky chirped, drawing both their attention. She was sitting on the floor and seemed to have rabbits sprouting everywhere, including one peeking out from the leg of her pink corduroy overalls.

Alarm crossed Noah's face. "The bunnies have to stay here," he said firmly.

Her tiny lip pouted out. "Go."

"Would you like some bunnies?" Moon Bright asked. She smiled at Becky.

Starr stepped forward. "Mother," she warned.

"It's all right, dear. We have lots of rabbits, and they're old enough to take care of themselves."

"But—"

"And they make wonderful pets for children," Blue River added. He smiled happily. "They rarely bite, you know. Becky can have all the bunnies she wants."

At that precise moment Noah suspected Moon Bright and Blue River weren't as guileless as they appeared. His eyes narrowed. They disapproved of him—*a doctor*—as a potential mate for Starr. Could this be revenge for his supposed friendship with their daughter?

No.

What was he thinking? They weren't that kind of people. Besides, it didn't matter anyway. Becky had made up her mind, unless he could make her listen to reason.

Noah knelt next to his niece. "Sweetheart, Kitty and the bunnies won't get along. They'll be much happier here."

For a second she seemed doubtful. "O'ood Kitty?"

"Right, Kitty's good, but the bunnies might be afraid. He's a lot bigger than they are."

Not to mention well equipped with fangs and claws. Kitty spent hours each day chattering at the seagulls—he'd probably have heart failure at the sight of six tasty little bunnies.

After a brief deliberation, the child shook her head. "O'ood Kitty. Bunnies, go."

Damn.

"All right. They can go home with us." He felt Starr's incredulous stare, and winced.

"Noah!"

"Never mind," he muttered.

He didn't even look at Starr as they discussed ways to contain the rabbits while being transported. Moon Bright and Blue River weren't a lot of help; they made several suggestions, each more impractical than the last. It was Starr who solved the problem, fetching an enormous old suitcase and ruthlessly punching air holes on the top and sides. The holes were just big enough for Becky to stick her fingers through, giggling when the inquisitive animals sniffed at them.

"You'll need food and bedding," Blue River said. He carried several large sacks from a shed in the backyard and loaded them into the trunk, all the while offering advice about building a hutch and explaining that a rabbit can have bunnies every thirty days. Wasn't that remarkable?

Everything was done with a good-natured bonhomie, as though they couldn't be rude to anyone, not even to the *doctor* they feared might marry their daughter…heaven forbid.

Noah mumbled a thank-you and started the car. He drove staring straight ahead, not daring to turn in Starr's direction. After a couple of minutes he heard a low choking sound.

"Is something wrong?"

Starr began to laugh.

"It isn't funny," Noah growled. He kept having visions of rabbits, multiplying exponentially.

"It's hysterical from my vantage point," she said cheerfully.

He looked at her, all soft and smiling and flushed with humor, and smiled himself. Suddenly, acquiring six rabbits